THIS BOOK
BELONGS TO:

_____

_____

Tales of
Pirates and
Buccaneers

CHILDREN'S CLASSICS

This unique series of Children's Classics™ features accessible and highly readable texts paired with the work of talented and brilliant illustrators of bygone days to create fine editions for today's parents and children to rediscover and treasure. Besides being a handsome addition to any home library, this series features genuine bonded-leather spines stamped in gold, full-color illustrations, and high-quality acid-free paper that will enable these books to be passed from one generation to the next.

Adventures of Huckleberry Finn
The Adventures of Tom Sawyer
Aesop's Fables
Alice's Adventures in Wonderland
Andersen's Fairy Tales
Anne of Avonlea
Anne of Green Gables
At the Back of the North Wind
Black Beauty
The Call of the Wild
A Child's Book of Country Stories
A Child's Book of Stories
A Child's Book of Stories from
    Many Lands
A Child's Christmas
A Christmas Carol and Other
    Christmas Stories
Cinderella and Other Classic
    Italian Fairy Tales
The Complete Mother Goose
Goldilocks and the Three Bears
    and Other Classic English Fairy
    Tales
Great Dog Stories
Grimm's Fairy Tales
Hans Brinker *or* The Silver Skates

Heidi
The Hound of the Baskervilles
The Jungle Book
Just So Stories
Kidnapped
King Arthur and His Knights
A Little Child's Book of Stories
Little Men
The Little Princess
Little Women
Peter Pan
Rebecca of Sunnybrook Farm
Robin Hood
Robinson Crusoe
The Secret Garden
The Sleeping Beauty and Other
    Classic French Fairy Tales
The Swiss Family Robinson
Tales from Shakespeare
Tales of Pirates and Buccaneers
Through the Looking Glass and
    What Alice Found There
Treasure Island
A Very Little Child's Book of
    Stories
The Wind in the Willows

Tales of Pirates and Buccaneers

Written and Illustrated by
Howard Pyle

Edited by Gregory R. Suriano

CHILDREN'S CLASSICS
New York • Avenel

This 1994 edition is published by Children's Classics, a division of dilithium
Press, Ltd., distributed by Random House Value Publishing, Inc.,
40 Engelhard Avenue, Avenel, New Jersey 07001.

DILITHIUM is a registered trademark and CHILDREN'S CLASSICS is a trademark of
dilithium Press, Ltd.

Printed and bound in the United States of America

Library of Congress Cataloging-in-Publication Data
Pyle, Howard, 1853-1911.
Tales of pirates and buccaneers / written and illustrated by Howard Pyle; edited, with
an introduction, by Gregory R. Suriano.
       p. cm.
    Contents: The buccaneers — The fate of a treasure-town — The ghost of Captain
Brand — Buccaneers and marooners of the Spanish Main — The ruby of Kishmoor —
Captain Scarfield —Tom Chist and the treasure-box.
    ISBN 0-517-10162-9
    Children's stories, American. 2. Pirates—Juvenile fiction. 3. Buccaneers—
Juvenile fiction. [1. Pirates—Fiction. 2. Buccaneers—Fiction. 3. Short stories.]
I. Suriano, Gregory R., 1951- . II. Title.
PZ7.P993Tal 1994
[Fic] —dc20
                                                                              93-44689
                                                                                    CIP
                                                                                     AC

8 7 6 5 4 3

Editor's Note. The stories and illustrations in this book were originally created a
century ago, and much of the text is based on historical incidents and real persons.
Any offense to modern sensibilities as may occur is unintentional and does not reflect
the attitudes of the editor or publisher of this book.

Contents

List of Color Illustrations

Introduction

Howard Pyle has achieved lasting fame as the father of American illustration, but he was also a superb storyteller. And although he is well known as the author and illustrator of such children's classics as *The Merry Adventures of Robin Hood* and *The Story of King Arthur and His Knights*, many of Pyle's stories, particularly those based on historical incidents, appeal to people of all ages.

Born in 1853 in Wilmington, Delaware, Howard Pyle was the eldest of four children in a Quaker family. As a boy he loved the fantastic adventures he read in *Grimm's German Fairy Tales*, *The Arabian Nights*, and Nathaniel Hawthorne's *The Wonder Book*, and he eagerly pored over picture books and the illustrations in American and British magazines. When he was sixteen, he began three years of study at a Philadelphia art school. He spent his early twenties working in his father's leather business in Wilmington and improving his writing and drawing skills. In 1876, encouraged by the publication of some of his work in two important magazines, he moved to New York City.

Like many of the best artists of his day, much of Pyle's art was created for popular magazines. After his arrival in New York, he made steady progress in getting illustration assignments from such periodicals as *St. Nicholas* and *Harper's Monthly*. In the following decades, the Harper publishing empire would print many of Pyle's stories and illustrations in their magazines and books.

Pyle's reputation grew during the three years he lived in New York, as his stories, articles, and drawings, which were usually of an historical nature, appeared regularly in magazines. For the Christmas 1878 issue of *Harper's Weekly*, Pyle did an illustration entitled "Christmas Morning in Old New York," and to ensure its historical accuracy, he collected period costumes. That was the beginning of his collection of authentic American costumes, which constantly expanded and became one of the largest and most valuable in the country.

For his early realistic and historical illustrations, Pyle created watercolor paintings, which were engraved on wood so they could be printed by the methods of the day. After the advent of new photomechanical techniques for reproducing art, he painted his illustrations in oils, and these were reproduced directly in all their tones and colors.

Pyle returned to Wilmington for good in 1879, and during the next twenty years his fame as a writer and an artist spread. For magazines he illustrated his own articles and stories, as well as those written by others; for *Harper's Monthly*, for example, he contributed pen-and-ink drawings for a series of articles on George Washington by another, future, president, Woodrow Wilson. His books for children—*Pepper and Salt, The Merry Adventures of Robin Hood, The Wonder Clock, Otto of the Silver Hand*, and others—were critical and popular successes and set the standard for the quality design of children's books in America.

In 1881 Pyle married Anne Poole in a Quaker wedding; their family eventually included six children. It was at the Pyles' summer home in Chadds Ford, Pennsylvania, that the famous Brandywine art school took shape. Pyle first began teaching at the Drexel Institute of Art, Science, and Industry in Philadelphia in 1894. He was a born teacher, and his aim was nothing less than to revolutionize the teaching of art in the same way that he had revolutionized the illustration of books. In the summer of 1898 he established a program that allowed students from Drexel to study in the country and paint realistically—not from studio models, but with the stimulus of outdoor scenes and light. Beginning in 1900, Pyle inspired, dazzled, and educated eager students at his own school at Chadds Ford, on the banks of the Brandywine River. American art in the twentieth century has been graced by the images of many of Pyle's pupils, including N.C. Wyeth, Maxfield Parrish, Jessie Willcox Smith, Frank Schoonover, and Violet Oakley.

In 1907, Pyle became an enthusiastic mural painter, and the creation of these panoramas was well suited to his expertise in illustrating historical scenes. When, in order to study the murals of the Italian Renaissance masters, he traveled with his family to Italy in 1910, he was already experiencing bouts of ill health. A year later he died of a kidney infection in Florence, the world's most extraordinary city of art.

Howard Pyle was interested in many periods of history—the Revolutionary War era, the Middle Ages, the pirate days of the seventeenth and eighteenth centuries. He wrote numerous tales based on these exciting times. Many of his books were set in the Middle Ages, including the King Arthur series (four books beginning with *The Story of King Arthur and His Knights* in 1903) and the classic picture books *Otto of the Silver Hand* and *The Wonder Clock*. All are beautifully designed and feature black-and-white drawings reminiscent of old woodcuts. His exciting and famous novel of medieval knighthood, *Men of Iron*, was published in 1892.

The American Revolution also inspired Pyle illustrations, such as those he did for *Yankee Doodle* and Oliver Wendell Holmes's *Dorothy Q, A Ballad of the Boston Tea Party,* and *Grandmother's Story of Bunker Hill Battle.* A majority of his illustrations of Revolutionary War days appeared, however, in such popular magazines of the time as *St. Nicholas, Harper's Monthly, The Century Magazine, Scribner's Monthly,* and *Harper's Young People.* It was for these and other publications that Pyle wrote and illustrated most of his tales of pirates and buccaneers.

Howard Pyle was fascinated by pirates and tales of adventure and intrigue set in exotic places. And he applied the same intensity of historical research to the writing of his pirate stories and articles that he brought to his art. While some of the tales may center around fictional heroes and events, they are all based on true accounts of the days when colorful and dangerous treasure-hunters ruled the waters of the Atlantic and the Caribbean.

Collected in this book—and edited for modern readers—are seven of Howard Pyle's exciting pirate tales, illustrated with his black-and-white and full-color illustrations, all of which originally appeared in magazines from 1887 to 1907. In such stories as "The Buccaneers," "The Ghost of Captain Brand," "The Ruby of Kishmoor," and "Tom Chist and the Treasure-Box," Pyle's main characters are young men who thirst for adventure or unexpectedly find themselves embroiled in mysterious events, insidious plots, and dangerous escapades. They perform heroically in the temporary company of pirates and often fall under the spell of an enchanting young lady. Through these stories walk such great and frightening pirates as Captain Kidd, Blackbeard, and Captain Morgan. The settings for these fabulous adventures of centuries past are the exotic, and often lawless, Spanish islands and colonies in the New World—places like Cartagena, Hispaniola, Tortuga, Panama, and Portobello.

In *Tales of Pirates and Buccaneers*, Howard Pyle, the master illustrator and skilled teller of historical-adventure stories, places his young heroes in the path of danger and excitement. In exciting tropical lands, on the high seas and on ships roaring with cannons and flying the skull and crossbones, they meet the most dangerous swashbucklers, freebooters, marooners, outlaws, thieves, treasure-seekers, plunderers, buccaneers, and pirate captains ever to infest the seven seas.

Gregory R. Suriano

Avenel, New Jersey
1994

Tales of
Pirates and
Buccaneers

The Buccaneers

I

In the year 1664 Harry Mostyn's father embarked from Portsmouth, in England, for Barbados, where he owned a large sugar plantation. To those parts of America he transported with himself his whole family, of whom Harry was the fifth of eight children —a great robust fellow as little fitted for the church (for which he was being educated) as could be. At the time of this story, though not above sixteen years old, Harry Mostyn was as big and well-grown as many a man of twenty, and of such a reckless and dare-devil spirit that no adventure was too dangerous or too mischievous for him to embark upon.

At this time there was a deal of talk in those parts of the Americas concerning Captain Morgan, and the successes he was having pirating against the Spaniards.

This man had once been an indentured servant with Mr. Rolls, a sugar broker in Barbados. Having served out his time, and being of lawless disposition, possessing also an appetite for adventure, he joined with others of his kind and, purchasing a sailing ship of three guns, embarked upon a career of piracy that became the most successful that ever was heard of in the world.

Harry had known this man very well when he was serving as a

clerk at Mr. Rolls's sugar wharf. He was a tall, broad-shouldered, strapping fellow, with red cheeks, thick red lips, rolling blue eyes, and hair as red as any chestnut. Many knew him for a bold, gruff-spoken man, but no one at that time suspected that he had it in him to become so famous as he afterward grew to be.

The fame of his exploits had been the talk of those parts for more than a year, when, in the latter part of 1665, Captain Morgan, having made a successful expedition against the Spaniards into the Gulf of Campeche—where he took several important purchases from the silver-and-gold-coin fleet—came to Barbados to fit out another such venture and to enlist recruits.

He and certain other adventurers had purchased a vessel of some five hundred tons, which they proposed to convert into a pirate ship by cutting portholes for cannon and running three or four short-nosed cannons across her main deck. The name of this ship was the *Good Samaritan*, as ill-fitting a name as could be for such a craft, which, instead of being designed for the healing of wounds, was intended to inflict such devastation as those wicked men proposed.

Here was a piece of mischief exactly fitted to our young Harry Mostyn's tastes; and having made up a bundle of clothes, and with not more than a shilling in his pocket, he made an excursion into the town to seek Captain Morgan. There he found the great pirate established at a tavern, with a little court of ragamuffins and swashbucklers gathered about him, all talking loudly, and drinking healths in raw rum as though it were sugared water.

And what a fine figure the buccaneer had become! How different from the poor, humble clerk who worked at the sugar wharf! What a deal of gold braid! What a fine silver-hilted Spanish sword! What a magnificent velvet sling, hung with three silver-mounted pistols! If Harry's mind had not been made up before, certainly such a spectacle of glory would have determined it.

Harry asked Captain Morgan to step aside with him, and when they went into a corner, explained that he wanted to enlist as a gentleman adventurer upon this expedition. The rogue of a buccaneer captain burst out laughing, and giving Harry a great thump upon the back, swore that he would make a man of him and that it was a pity to make a parson out of so good a piece of stuff.

Captain Morgan was as good as his word. When the *Good Samaritan* set sail with a favoring wind for the island of Jamaica, Harry found himself established as one of the adventurers aboard.

II

The town of Port Royal in the year 1665 was a sight well worth looking upon. There were no fine houses at that time, and no great counting-houses built of brick, such as may be found nowadays. There was a crowd of board-and-wattle huts huddled along the streets, all enlivened with flags and bits of color. To this place came all the pirates and buccaneers that infested those parts, and men shouted and swore and gambled, and poured out money like water, and then, perhaps, wound up their merrymaking by dying of fever. For the sky in these torrid latitudes is full of clouds overhead, and as hot as any blanket, and when the sun shone forth it streamed down upon the smoking sands so that the houses were ovens and the streets were furnaces; it was little wonder that men died like rats in a hole. But little they appeared to care for that. Everywhere could be seen a multitude of painted women and merchants and pirates, gaudy with red scarfs and gold braid and all sorts of odds and ends of foolish finery, all fighting and gambling and bartering for that ill-gotten treasure of the berobed Spaniard.

Here, arriving, Captain Morgan found a hearty welcome, and a message from the governor awaiting him. The message bid him to attend His Excellency at the earliest possible occasion. So, taking Harry (of whom he had grown very fond) along with him, the pirate went, without any loss of time, to visit Sir Thomas Modiford, who was then the royal governor of all this devil's brew of wickedness.

They found His Excellency seated in a great easy chair, under the shadow of a slatted veranda, the floor of which was paved with brick. He was clad, for the sake of coolness, only in his shirt, breeches, and stockings, and he wore slippers on his feet. He was smoking a great cigar and a goblet of lime juice and water and rum stood at his elbow on a table. Here, out of the glare of the heat, it was all very cool and pleasant, with a sea breeze blowing violently in through the slats, setting them rattling now and then, and stirring Sir Thomas's long hair, which he had pushed back for the sake of coolness.

The purpose of this interview concerned the rescue of one Le Sieur Simon, who, with his wife and daughter, was held captive by the Spaniards.

This gentleman adventurer, Le Sieur Simon, had, a few years before, been set up by the buccaneers as governor of the island of Saint Catherine. This place, though well fortified by the Spaniards, had been seized upon by the buccaneers, who established themselves there, and so infested the commerce of those seas that no Spanish fleet was safe from them. At last the Spaniards, no longer able to endure these assaults, sent a great force against the pirates to drive them out of their island stronghold. This they did, retaking Saint Catherine, together with its governor, his wife, and daughter, as well as the whole garrison of buccaneers.

The conquerors sent some of these buccaneers to the galleys, some to the mines, some to no man knows where. The governor himself—Le Sieur Simon—was to be sent to Spain, there to stand trial for piracy.

The news of all this had only just been received in Jamaica, having been brought there by a Spanish captain, Don Roderiguez Sylvia, who was also the bearer of dispatches to the Spanish authorities that related the whole affair.

As Harry and the captain walked back together from the governor's house to the tavern where they were staying, the buccaneer assured his companion that his idea was to obtain those dispatches from the Spanish captain that very afternoon, even if he had to use force to seize them.

All this was undertaken only because of the friendship that the governor and Captain Morgan had for Le Sieur Simon. And, indeed, it was wonderful how honest and how faithful were these wicked men in their dealings with one another. For Governor Modiford and Le Sieur Simon and the buccaneers were all of one kind—all taking a share in the piracies of those times, and all holding by one another as though they were the most honest men in the world. So it was they were all so determined to rescue Le Sieur Simon from the Spaniards.

III

Having reached the tavern after his interview with the governor, Captain Morgan found there a number of his companions, such as usually gathered at that place to be in attendance upon him. Some were from the *Good Samaritan*; others hoped to obtain benefits from him; others were ragamuffins who gathered around him because he was famous and because it pleased them to be called his followers. A successful pirate almost always had such a little court surrounding him.

Finding a dozen or more of these rascals gathered there, Captain Morgan informed them of his present plan—that he was going to find the Spanish captain to demand his papers of him—and he invited them to accompany him.

With this following at his heels, the buccaneer started off down the street, his lieutenant, a Cornishman named Bartholomew Davis, upon one hand and Harry Mostyn upon the other. So they paraded the streets for the best part of an hour before they found the Spanish captain. For whether he had got wind that Captain Morgan was searching for him, or whether, finding himself in a place so full of his enemies, he had buried himself in some place of hiding, it is certain that the buccaneers had traveled across almost the whole town before they discovered that he was staying at an inn kept by a Portuguese. There they went, and there Captain Morgan entered with the utmost coolness and composure, his followers crowding noisily in at his heels.

The space within was very dark, being lighted only by the doorway and by two large slatted windows or openings in the front.

In this dark, hot place—not overroomy at the best—were twelve or fifteen villanous-looking men, sitting at tables and drinking together, waited upon by the innkeeper and his wife. Harry had no trouble discovering which of this lot of men was Captain Sylvia, for not only did Captain Morgan direct his angry glance upon him, but the Spaniard was dressed with more care and with more show of finery than any of the others who were there.

Captain Morgan approached him and demanded his papers, and the other replied with such a jabber of Spanish and English that no man present understood what he said. To this Captain Morgan replied that he must have those papers, no matter what it might cost him to obtain them, and then drew a pistol from his sling and presented it at the other's head.

At this threatening action the innkeeper's wife fell screaming, and her husband, in a frenzy, begged them not to tear the house down about his ears.

Harry Mostyn could hardly tell what followed, only that all of a sudden there was a great uproar of combat. Knives flashed everywhere, and then a pistol was fired so close to his head that he was stunned, hearing someone crying out in a loud voice, but not knowing whether it was a friend or a foe who had been shot. Then another pistol shot so deafened what was left of Harry's hearing that his ears rang for more than an hour afterward. By this time the whole place was full of gunpowder smoke, and there was the sound of blows and oaths and cries and the clashing of knives.

As Harry, who had no stomach for such fighting, and no very particular interest in the quarrel, was making for the door, a little Portuguese, as withered and as nimble as an ape, came ducking under the table and plunged at his stomach with a great long knife, which, had it landed as intended, would surely have ended his adventures then and there. Finding himself in such danger, Harry picked up a heavy chair, and, flinging it at his enemy, who was preparing for another attack, he fairly ran for it out of the door, expecting at any moment to feel the thrust of the blade between his ribs.

A considerable crowd was gathered outside, and others, hearing the uproar, were coming running to join them. With these Harry stood, trembling like a leaf, and with cold chills running like water up and down his back at the narrow escape from the danger that had threatened him.

While sixteen-year-old Harry stood there trying to recover his composure and the fighting continued within, suddenly two men came running almost together out the door, a crowd of the combatants at their heels. The first of these men was Captain Sylvia; the other, who was pursuing him, was Captain Morgan.

As the crowd about the door parted before the sudden appearance of these two, the Spanish captain, seeing what he supposed was a way of escape opened to him, darted across the street with incredible swiftness toward an alleyway at the other side. Seeing his prey likely to get away from him, Captain Morgan snatched a pistol out of his sling, and resting it for an instant across his arm, fired at the flying Spaniard—with so true an aim that, though the street was now full of people, the other went tumbling over and over in a heap in the alley, where he lay, after a twitch or two, as still as a log.

At the sound of the shot and the fall of the man, the crowd scattered upon all sides, yelling and screaming. Since the street was pretty clear, Captain Morgan ran across to where his victim lay, his smoking pistol still in his hand, and Harry following close at his heels.

Poor Harry had never before beheld a man killed thus in an instant, who a moment before had been so full of life and activity. When Captain Morgan turned the body over upon its back Harry could see at a glance, little as he knew of such matters, that the man was stone dead. And indeed it was a dreadful sight for him who was hardly more than a child. He stood rooted for he knew not how long, his fingers twitching and his limbs shuddering, staring down at the dead face. Meanwhile, a great crowd was gathering about them again.

As for Captain Morgan, he went about his work with the utmost coolness and deliberation imaginable. With fingers that neither twitched nor shook, he unbuttoned the waistcoat and the shirt of the man he had murdered. There were a gold cross and a bunch of silver medals hung by a whipcord about the neck of the dead man.

This Captain Morgan broke away with a snap, handing the jingling baubles to Harry, who took them in his nerveless hand and fingers that he could hardly close upon what they held.

The papers Captain Morgan found in a wallet in an inner breastpocket of the Spaniard's waistcoat. These he examined one by one. Finding them to his satisfaction, he tied them up again, and slipped the wallet and its contents into his own pocket.

Then for the first time he appeared to observe Harry, who, indeed, must have made the perfect picture of horror and dismay. Bursting out laughing, and slipping the pistol he had used back into its sling again, he hit poor Harry a great slap upon the back, bidding him be a man, for he would see many such sights as this.

But, indeed, it was no laughing matter for poor Harry, for it was many days before his imagination could rid itself of the image of the dead Spaniard's face. And as he walked down the street with his companions—leaving the crowd behind them, and the dead body where it lay for its friends to look after, his ears humming and ringing from the deafening noise of the pistol shots fired in the close room, and the sweat trickling down his face in drops—he knew not whether all that had passed had been real, or whether it was all a dream from which he might presently awaken.

IV

The papers Captain Morgan had seized upon as the fruit of the murder he had committed must have been as perfectly satisfactory to him as could be, for having paid a second visit that evening to Governor Modiford, the pirate lifted anchor the next morning, and made sail toward the Gulf of Darien. There, after cruising about in those waters for above a fortnight without falling in with a vessel of any sort, at the end of that time they overtook a ship bound from Portobelo to Cartagena. They took the vessel, and finding her loaded with nothing better than raw hides, they sunk her, being then about twenty leagues from the main of Cartagena. From the captain of this vessel they learned that the silver-and-gold fleet was then lying in the harbor of Portobelo, not yet having set sail, but waiting for the change of the winds before embarking for Spain. Besides this, which was a good deal more to their purpose, the

Spaniards told the pirates that Le Sieur Simon, his wife, and daughter were confined aboard the flagship of that fleet, and that the name of that ship was the *Santa Maria y Valladolid*.

As soon as Captain Morgan had obtained the information he desired, he directed his course straight for the Bay of Santo Blaso. There he could lie safely within the cape of that name without any danger of discovery (that part of the mainland being entirely uninhabited) and yet be within twenty or twenty-five leagues of Portobelo.

Having come safely to this anchorage, he at once declared his intentions to his companions. He explained that it was entirely impossible for them to hope to sail their vessel into the harbor of Portobelo, and to attack the Spanish flagship where it lay in the midst of the armed fleet; therefore, if anything was to be accomplished, it must be undertaken by some subtle design rather than by open-handed boldness. Having so prefaced what he had to say, the captain now declared that it was his purpose to take one of the ship's boats and to go in that to Portobelo, trusting for some opportunity to occur to aid him either in the accomplishment of his aims or in the gaining of some further information. He then invited any who dared to do so to volunteer for the expedition, telling them plainly that he would force no man to go against his will, for at best it was a desperate enterprise, possessing only the recommendation that in its achievement the few who undertook it would gain great renown, and perhaps considerable booty.

And such was the incredible influence of this bold man over his companions, and such was their confidence in his skill and cunning, that not above a dozen of all those aboard hung back from the undertaking, but nearly every man desired to go.

Of these volunteers Captain Morgan chose twenty—among others Harry Mostyn—and having arranged with his lieutenant that if nothing was heard from the expedition at the end of three days he should sail for Jamaica to await news, he embarked upon that enterprise, which was perhaps the boldest and the most desperate of all those that have since made his name so famous. For what could be a more unparalleled undertaking than for a little open boat, containing but twenty men, to enter the harbor of the third-strongest fortress of the Spanish mainland with the intention of cutting out the Spanish flagship from the midst of a whole fleet of powerfully armed vessels. How many men in all the world do you suppose would attempt such a thing?

But there is this to be said of that great buccaneer: that if he undertook enterprises so desperate as this, he yet laid his plans so well that they never went altogether wrong. Moreover, the very desperation of his successes was of such a nature that no man could suspect that he would dare to undertake such things; therefore, his enemies were never prepared to guard against his attacks. Had he but worn the king's colors and served under the rules of honest war, he might have become as great and as renowned as Admiral Blake himself!

Captain Morgan in this open boat with his twenty mates reached the Cape of Salmedina toward the fall of day. Arriving within view of the harbor they discovered the silver-and-gold fleet at anchor, with two men-of-war and an armed galley riding as a guard at the mouth of the harbor, barely half a league distant from the other ships. Having spied the fleet in this position, the pirates pulled down their sails and rowed along the coast, feigning to be a Spanish vessel from Nembre de Dios. So hugging the shore, they boldly entered the harbor, on the opposite side of which might be seen the fortress some distance away.

Having now come so near to the climax of their adventure, Captain Morgan required every man to make an oath to stand by him to the last, and Harry Mostyn swore as heartily as any man aboard —although his heart was beating at a great rate at the approach of what was to happen. Having thus received the oaths of all his followers, Captain Morgan commanded the surgeon of the expedition when the order was given to bore six holes in the boat, so that, it sinking under them, they might all be compelled to push forward, with no chance of retreat. And such was the power of this man over his followers, and such was their awe of him, that not one of them uttered even so much as a murmur, though what he had commanded the surgeon to do pledged them either to victory or to death, with no chance to choose between. Nor did the surgeon question the orders he had received or even dream of disobeying them.

By now dusk had fallen. Spying two fishermen in a canoe at a little distance, Captain Morgan demanded of them in Spanish which vessel of those at anchor in the harbor was the flagship, for he had dispatches for its captain. The fishermen, suspecting nothing, pointed out a galleon of great size riding at anchor not half a league distant.

Toward this vessel the pirates directed their course, and when they had come pretty near, Captain Morgan called to the surgeon that now it was time for him to perform the duty that had been required of him. Then the surgeon did as he was ordered, and did it so thoroughly that the water soon came gushing into the boat in great streams, and all hands pulled for the galleon as though every moment was to be their last.

Like all in the boat, Harry Mostyn's awe of Captain Morgan was so great that he would rather have gone to the bottom than have questioned his command, even when it was to sink the boat. Nevertheless, when he felt the cold water gushing about his feet (for he had taken off his shoes and stockings) he became possessed with such a fear of being drowned that even the Spanish galleon had no terrors for him if he could only feel its solid planks beneath his feet.

Indeed, all the crew appeared to be possessed of a like fear, for they pulled at the oars with such an incredible force that they were under the quarter of the galleon before the boat was half filled with water.

As they approached—it then being pretty dark and the moon not yet having risen—the watch upon the deck hailed them, and Captain Morgan called out in Spanish that he was Captain Alvarez Mendazo, and that he brought despatches for the flagship.

But at that moment, the boat, which was quite full of water, suddenly tilted upon one side as though to sink beneath them. Then all hands, without further orders, went scrambling up the side as nimble as so many monkeys, each armed with a pistol in one hand and a cutlass in the other, and so were upon deck before the watch could collect his wits to utter any outcry or to give any other alarm than to cry out, "Bless us! Who are these?"—at which words somebody knocked him down with the butt of a pistol, though who it was Harry could not tell in the darkness and the hurry.

Before any of those upon deck could recover from their alarm or those from below come up upon deck, some of the pirates, under the carpenter and the surgeon, had run to the gun-room and had taken possession of the arms, while Captain Morgan, with Harry and a Portuguese called Murillo Braziliano, had flown with the speed of the wind into the great cabin.

Here they found the captain of the flagship playing cards with Le Sieur Simon and a friend, Madam Simon and her daughter being present.

Captain Morgan instantly aimed his pistol at the breast of the Spanish captain, swearing, with a most horrible fierce expression on his face, that if he spoke a word or made any outcry he was a dead man. As for Harry, having now got his hand into the game, he performed the same service for the Spaniard's friend, declaring he would shoot him dead if he opened his lips or lifted so much as a single finger.

All this occurred while the ladies, not comprehending what had happened, had sat as mute as stones. But now having so far recovered themselves as to find a voice, the younger of the two started screaming, at which Le Sieur Simon called out to her to be still, for these were friends who had come to help them, and not enemies who had come to harm them.

All this occupied only a little while, for in less than a minute three or four of the pirates had come into the cabin, who, together with the Portuguese, proceeded at once to bind the two Spaniards hand and foot, and to gag them. This being done to the buccaneer's satisfaction, and the Spanish captain being stretched out in the corner of the cabin, he instantly cleared his face of its terrible expression, and bursting forth into a great loud laugh, clapped his hand to Le Sieur Simon's, which he wrung with the best will in the world. Having done this, and being in a fine humor after this his first success, he turned to the two ladies. "And this, ladies," said he, taking Harry by the hand and presenting him, "is a young gentleman who has embarked with me to learn the trade of piracy. I recommend him to your politeness."

What confusion this caused for Harry, who at his best was never easy in the company of strange ladies! What must have been his emotions to find himself introduced to the attention of Madam Simon and her daughter—he being in his bare feet, clad only in his shirt and breeches, with no hat upon his head, a pistol in one hand and a cutlass in the other! However, he was not left for long to his embarrassments, for almost immediately after he had relaxed, Captain Morgan suddenly became serious again: bidding Le Sieur Simon to get his ladies away into some place of safety—for the most hazardous part of this adventure was yet to occur—he left the cabin with Harry and the other pirates at his heels.

Having come upon deck, Harry beheld that a part of the Spanish crew were huddled forward in a flock like so many sheep (the others being crowded below with the hatches fastened upon them), and such was the terror of the pirates, and so dreadful the name of Henry Morgan, that not one of those poor wretches dared to lift up his voice to give any alarm, nor even to attempt an escape by jumping overboard.

At Captain Morgan's orders, these men, together with certain of his own company, began setting the sails, which, the night now having fallen, was not for a good while observed by any of the vessels riding at anchor around them.

Indeed, the pirates might have made good their escape, with at most only a shot or two from the men-of-war, had it not then been the full of the moon, which, having arisen, revealed to those of the fleet that lay closest around them what was being done aboard the flagship.

At this, one of the vessels hailed them. After a while, having no reply, it hailed them again. Even then the Spaniards might not immediately have suspected anything was wrong, but only that the flagship, for some reason best known to itself, was shifting his anchorage, had not one of the Spaniards aloft—but who it was Captain Morgan was never able to discover—answered the hail by crying out that the flagship had been seized by the pirates.

The alarm was instantly given and the mischief done, for at once there was a tremendous bustle through that part of the fleet lying nearest the flagship—a shouting of orders, a beating of drums, and the running back and forth of the crews.

But by this time the sails of the flagship had filled with a strong land breeze that was blowing up the harbor; and after the carpenter, at Captain Morgan's orders, cut away both anchors, the galleon traveled up the harbor, gathering headway every moment with the wind nearly dead astern. The nearest vessel was the only one that for the moment was able to offer any opposition. This ship, having by this time cleared away one of its guns, was able to fire a parting shot against the flagship, striking her somewhere forward, as Harry could see by a great shower of splinters that flew up in the moon-light.

At the sound of the shot all the vessels of the fleet not yet disturbed by the alarm were aroused at once, so that the pirates had the satisfaction of knowing that they would have to run the gauntlet of all the ships between them and the open sea before they could consider themselves escaped.

And indeed to Harry's mind it seemed that the battle which followed must have been the most terrific artillery bombardment that ever the world beheld. It was not so great at first, for it was some while before the Spaniards could get their guns clear for action, they being not the least in the world prepared for such an occasion as this. But soon, first one and then another ship opened fire upon the galleon, until it seemed to Harry that all the thunders of heaven let loose upon them could not have created a greater uproar, and that it was not possible that any of them could escape destruction.

By now the moon had risen full and round, so that the clouds of smoke that rose in the air appeared as white as snow. The air seemed full of the hiss and screaming of shot, each one of which, when it struck the galleon, was magnified by Harry's imagination into ten times its real strength from the crash which it delivered, and from the cloud of splinters it would cast up into the moon-light. At last he suddenly beheld one poor man knocked sprawling across the deck, who, as he raised his arm from behind the mast, disclosed that the hand was gone from it, and that the shirt sleeve was red with blood in the moonlight. At this sight all the strength fell away from poor Harry, and he felt sure that a similar fate, or even a worse one, must be in store for him.

But, after all, this was nothing to what it might have been in broad daylight, for what with the darkness of night, and the little

The Buccaneers

The Fate of a Treasure-Town

preparation the Spaniards could make for such a business, and the
extreme haste with which they discharged their guns (many not
understanding what was the cause of all this uproar), nearly all the
shot flew so wide of the mark that not above one in twenty struck
that at which it was aimed.

Meantime Captain Morgan, with Le Sieur Simon, who had followed him upon deck, stood just above where Harry lay behind the
shelter of the bulwark. The captain had lit a pipe of tobacco, and
he stood now in the bright moonlight close to the rail, with his
hands behind him, looking out ahead with the utmost coolness
imaginable, and paying no more attention to the din of battle than
if it were twenty leagues away. Now and then he would take his
pipe from his lips to utter an order to the man at the wheel. Except
for this he stood there hardly moving at all, the wind blowing his
long red hair over his shoulders.

Had it not been for the armed galley the pirates might have
gotten the galleon away with no great harm done in spite of all this
bombardment, for the man-of-war which rode at anchor nearest to
them at the mouth of the harbor was still so far away that they
might have passed it by hugging pretty close to the shore, without
any great harm being done to them in the darkness. But just at this
moment, when the open water lay in sight, came this galley pulling
out from behind the point of the shore in such a manner as either
to head the pirates off entirely, or else to compel them to approach
so near to the man-of-war that that latter vessel could discharge its
guns with greater effect.

This galley was like others of its kind found in these waters, the
hull being long and cut low to the water so as to allow the oars to
dip freely. The bow was sharp and projected far out ahead, mounting a swivel upon it, while at the stern a number of galleries built
one above another into a castle gave shelter to several companies of
musketeers as well as the officers commanding them.

Harry Mostyn could behold the approach of this galley from above the starboard bulwarks, and it appeared to him impossible for them to hope to escape either it or the man-of-war. But still Captain Morgan maintained the same composure that he had exhibited all the while, only now and then delivering an order to the man at the wheel, who, putting the helm over, threw the bows of the galleon around more to the larboard, as though to escape the bow of the galley and get into the open water beyond. This course brought the pirates ever closer and closer to the man-of-war, which now began to add its thunder to the din of the battle, and with so much more effect that at every discharge you might hear the crashing and crackling of splintered wood, and now and then the outcry or groaning of some man who was hurt. Indeed, had it been daylight, they would all have perished, but because of the darkness and the confusion and the hurry, they escaped entire destruction, though more by a miracle than through any policy upon their own part.

Meantime the galley, steering as though to come aboard of them, was now so near that it too began to open its musketry fire upon them, so that the humming and rattling of bullets were added to the noise of the cannons.

In two minutes more it would have been aboard of them, when Captain Morgan roared suddenly to the man at the helm to put it hard-a-starboard. In response the man ran the wheel over with the utmost quickness, and the galleon, obeying her helm very readily, came around upon a course which, if continued, would certainly bring them into collision with their enemy.

It is possible at first the Spaniards imagined the pirates intended to escape past their stern, for they instantly began backing oars to keep them from getting past, so that the water was all of a foam about them; at the same time they did this they poured in an immense fire of musketry.

As for Harry, for the moment he forgot all about everything else than as to whether or not his captain's maneuver would succeed, for in the very first moment he understood, as by some instinct, what Captain Morgan intended doing.

At this moment, so important in the execution of this plan, a bullet suddenly struck down the man at the wheel. Hearing the sharp outcry, Harry turned to see him fall forward, and then to his hands and knees upon the deck, the blood running in a black pool beneath him, while the wheel, escaping from his hands, spun over until the spokes were all a blur.

In an instant the ship would have fallen off before the wind had not Harry, leaping to the wheel (even as Captain Morgan shouted an order for someone to do so), seized the flying spokes, whirled them back again, and brought the bow of the galleon up to its former course.

In the first moment of this effort he had reckoned of nothing but of carrying out his captain's designs. He neither thought of cannon-balls nor of bullets. But now that his task was accomplished, he came suddenly back to himself to find the galleries of the galleon aflame with musket shots, and to became aware with a most horrible sinking of the spirits that all the shots were intended for him. He cast his eyes about him with despair, but no one came to ease him of his task, which, having undertaken, he had too much spirit to resign from carrying through to the end, though he was well aware that the very next instant might mean his sudden and violent death. His ears hummed and rang, and his brain swam as light as a feather. I know not whether he breathed, but he shut his eyes tightly, as though that might save him from the bullets that were raining about him.

At this moment the Spaniards must have discovered for the first time the pirates' design, for they suddenly ceased firing and began to shout out a multitude of orders, while the oars lashed at the water all about. But it was too late then for them to escape, for within a couple of seconds the galleon struck her enemy a blow so violent upon the larboard quarter as nearly to hurl Harry upon the deck. Then with a dreadful, horrible crackling of wood, commingled with a yelling of men's voices, the galley was swung around upon her side, and the galleon, sailing into the open sea, left nothing of her immediate enemy but a sinking wreck, and the water was dotted all over with waving hands in the moonlight.

And now, indeed, that all danger was past and gone, there were plenty to come running to help Harry at the wheel. As for Captain Morgan, having come down upon the main deck, he gave the young helmsman a slap upon the back. "Well, Master Harry," said he, "and did I not tell you I would make a man of you?" At this, poor Harry started laughing, but with a sad catch in his voice, for his hands trembled and were as cold as ice. As for his emotions, he was nearer crying than laughing, if Captain Morgan had but known it.

Nevertheless, though undertaken upon the spur of the moment, it was indeed a brave deed; and who knows how many young gentlemen of sixteen there are today who in a similar situation would act as well as Harry?

V

The balance of Harry Mostyn's adventures were of a lighter sort than those already recounted. The next morning, after the Spanish captain (a very polite and well-bred gentleman) had outfitted him with a suit of his own clothes, Harry was presented in a proper manner to the ladies. For Captain Morgan, if he had felt a liking for the young man before, could not now show sufficient regard for him. He ate in the great cabin and was praised by all. Madam Simon, who was a plump and red-faced lady, was forever praising him, and the young miss, who was extremely good-looking, was continually making eyes at him.

She and Harry would spend hours together, she making pretense of teaching him French, although he was so possessed with a passion of love that he was nearly suffocated with it. Perceiving his emotions, she responded with extreme good nature, so that had Harry been older, and the voyage proved longer, he might have become entirely overwhelmed by the charms of his fair siren. All this while the pirates were sailing straight for Jamaica, which they reached on the third day in perfect safety.

In that time, however, it is likely that the pirates had nearly gone crazy for joy; for when they came to examine their purchase they discovered her cargo to consist of silver and gold coins to the enormous sum of £130,000 in value. 'Twas a wonder they did not all

make themselves drunk for joy. No doubt they would have done so had not Captain Morgan, knowing they were still in the exact track of the Spanish fleets, threatened them that the first man among them who touched a drop of rum without his permission he would shoot him dead upon the deck. This threat had such effect that they all remained entirely sober until they had reached Port Royal Harbor, which they did about nine o'clock in the morning.

And now it was that Harry Mostyn's romance came all tumbling down about his ears. For they had hardly come to anchor in the harbor when a boat came from a man-of-war, and who should come stepping aboard but Lieutenant Grantley (a particular friend of

Harry's father) and his own eldest brother, Thomas, who, putting on a very stern face, informed Harry that he was a desperate and hardened villain who was sure to end at the gallows, and that he was to go immediately back to his home again. He told the young pirate apprentice that his family was greatly upset by his wickedness and ungrateful conduct. Nor could Harry move him from his inflexible purpose. "What," said Harry, "and will you not then let me wait until our prize is divided and I get my share?"

"Prize, indeed!" said his brother. "And do you then really think that your father would consent to your having a share in this terrible bloody and murdering business?"

And so, after a good deal of argument, Harry was convinced to go; and he did not even have an opportunity to say goodbye to the girl who had captured his heart. Nor did he see her anymore, except from a distance, she standing on the deck as he was rowed away from her, her face all stained with crying. For himself, he felt that there was no more joy in life. Nevertheless, standing up in the stern of the boat, he made an effort, though with an aching heart, to deliver her a fine bow with the hat he had borrowed from the Spanish captain, before his brother made him sit down again.

And so to the ending of this story, with only this to relate: that

Harry Mostyn, so far from going to the gallows, became in good time a respectable and wealthy sugar merchant, with an English wife and a fine family of children; and that, when the mood was upon him, he sometimes told the story of his adventures—and many others not here recounted, as well.

The Fate of
a Treasure-Town

A flaming tropical sky of blue, full of the heavy clouds of the
torrid zone; a wonderful sea of sapphire and emerald
color, creaming to white upon coral beaches; huge mountainous islands, fringed with cocoa-palms and crowned with exotic
plants; stagnant lagoons where the mangroves cover the oozing
mud with their dense green foliage, and where crawling, venomous
creatures move beneath the snaky roots. Flaming heat; blazing
light; teeming life; splendid color—and death lurking ever hidden
in the slime of the rivers. Such is nature's background to the life
that at one time filled the Spanish Main with the drift that floated
in broken fragments from the Old World to the New.

Place here and there in this setting of tropical luxuriance a semi-
medieval Spanish town—walled and fortified, built of stone and ce-
mented with concrete; place in these towns the old-time Spanish
life of Charles or Philip, blended with the life of another world; fill
the streets and plazas with the figures of hooded priests, armed
knights, swaggering soldiers, fair ladies half veiled, traders, assassins
—and then behold again an image of the days when the Spanish
Indies were in their glory.

At that time there floated upon those tropical seas great fleets of
slow-sailing galleons, carved, gilded, and painted—and around the

27

fleet there moved protecting war-galleys—crawling, centipedelike, across the face of the water, with oars for legs, while rows of slaves tugged and hauled beneath the cracking whip of the driver, and the captain and his officers sat high up, beneath the awning of the deck, drinking spiced wine and smoking cigars.

It was in such fleets as these that the gathered wealth of the Indies drifted across the western seas to Spain, to fill its leaking treasury with a constant stream from that wonderful New World of hidden mysteries and fabulous treasures.

Perhaps one of the convoys lags from the rest of the fleet. There comes skimming out from behind the fringed headland a lean, low boat full of half-naked cutthroats. It swoops down upon the derelict galleon like the falcon upon the wild goose, and soon the hollow flaming space of sky and sea is filled with the wildness of battle —the rattle of musket shots; the cracks of firelocks and pistols; the detonation of cannon; yells, shrieks, jeers, and curses. Clouds of pungent gunpowder smoke drift down the breeze, dissolving in the hot and reeking air, and under the cloud a crew of pirates swarm headlong over the rail and upon the deck of the galleon and finish

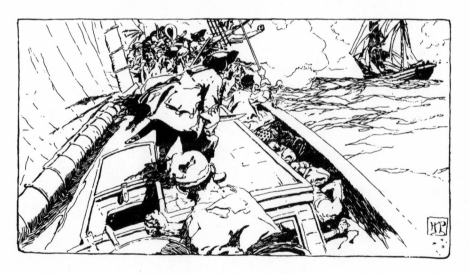

what they have begun. Afterward comes the silence of the completed work.

So those treasures of gold and silver and pearls and jewels were gathered in by Spain, and snatched from her again by the old buccaneers who sailed the Spanish Main.

A lonely island; a long strip of coral sand with waves bursting upon it; a shining mass of treasure poured out upon a sailcloth spread upon a beach; a circle of hungry-eyed, wolfish, unshaven, partly clad figures gathered about in the sunlight; the pirate chief standing over the booty—counting, adding, subtracting, parceling.

So the treasure was divided.

Then the panorama of life shifts again, and you see another sort of town than those Spanish strongholds of stonework and masonry —a town of thickly clustered houses, built of boards or twigs, smeared with mud; a network of narrow, filthy streets, each with a gutter down the middle full of stagnant slimy water; vultures brooding upon the poles in the sunlight, and a confusing sound of half-a-dozen languages making noisy the inns and taverns beneath. Such were the buccaneer towns of Port Royal and elsewhere, and there would gather a varied mass of humanity, skimmed from the cauldron of the Devil's brew in half-a-dozen countries of the earth. Here, stewing together in the heat, pirates, priests, money-changers, rumsellers, sailors, landsmen—male and female—drink and dice and dance and sweat till death grips them and wrings the life out of them.

In such stewpots of devilry the buccaneers spent the treasure that they looted from the Spaniards.

How incredible is the story of the wealth that flowed from the West Indies to Spain in those old days! It reads like a fairy tale. Half of Europe—and that, the richest half—poured its tribute into the treasury of Spain; yet it is estimated that one-third of the imperial revenue came to her from the West Indies.

It has never been told how vast was the treasure that was emptied from the New World into the Old in those days—the glorious days of Spanish power. We can only judge how great it was by similar evidence. The booties of Cortez and of Pizarro are famous in annals of New World history. In them we have read how the soldiers of the former carried away only a small part of the treasures looted at Mexico, yet were so loaded down with stolen gold that, when they fell into the lake in the memorable retreat from Mexico, they sank and drowned as though weighted with lead. Also we read how Pizarro exacted as a tribute for the liberation of the Inca Atahulpa people gold that filled to the depth of several feet a room seventeen feet wide by twenty-two feet long, and which was valued at 1,300,000 pesos d'or—the equivalent of nearly $15,500,000.

When Drake sailed the South Seas in the *Golden Hind* upon his piratical voyage in the years 1577–1579, and when he captured the *Nuestra Señora della Concepcion* (surnamed the *Cacafuego* or *Spitfire*) off Cape San Francisco, it took three days to transfer the treasure from the captured ship to his own. In that single haul there was realized a "purchase," as it was called, of over twenty-six tons of silver, besides eighty pounds of gold, thirteen chests of pieces of eight, and an enormous amount of jewels and gold and silver coins.

Upon the evidence of John Drake we read that when the *Golden Hind* laid her course for England by way of the Cape of Good Hope, she was so heavily filled with pure silver that she "rode exceeding deep in the water."

In this connection it may be said that when Captain Drake went from Plymouth to London to make his peace with the queen because of this and other piracies, he took with him, by way of a peace offering, a train of seven horses loaded with gold and silver coins and all his most precious jewels.

There is hardly a stretch of twenty miles of coast anywhere along the Spanish Main that does not hold a traditional treasure-ship sunk in three or four fathoms of clear warm water. Such sunken treasure is not merely a legend, for the sand-worn remnants of gold are still washed up from such a wreck upon the white beach of the Bay of Darien—worn fragments of chain, shapeless lumps of gold bullion, eroded disks of what were one time, perhaps, the gold and silver coins of Charles or Philip.

Such stories as these are the debris of fact that has drifted down the current of history from the wreck of the past to the present; they indicate some idea of the vast treasure that at one time poured into Spain from the wonderful New World of hundreds of years ago.

Let there be given a condition of human society in which there is no law to restrain the greed that lies hidden in the depths of the human soul. And given a limitless, incredible wealth of silver and gold to be had for the taking, with no more cost than a few human lives, a little blood, and maybe some smarting wounds, the result is to be expected.

Certain masterful men arose who taught the cattle-thieves of Tortuga and Hispaniola how easy and profitable it was to turn pirate and rob the Spaniards, and from then on no money-ship was safe from the buccaneers. All that was needed for such an occasion was a good boat, a musket, a supply of cartridges—these, and maybe a sword and a dagger, and the outfit was complete. If the venture was fortunate the pirate returned with pockets full of money and nothing to do but to spend it, with no thoughts of tomorrow; for there was plenty more to be had when this was gone. So the buccaneers came into the field and from then on the treasure from the West had to be carried to Spain in the great money-fleets before spoken of, guarded by war-galleys.

The accumulated treasure shipped by fleet to Spain was first gathered into certain fortified strongholds, where it was held for transshipment. These treasuries were two strongly walled and fortified cities commanding safe and ample harbors and guarded by armies of soldiers. One of these treasure-cities lay upon the west and the other upon the east of the dividing isthmus that stretches between the two oceans. The western reservoir was the old city of Panama; the eastern reservoir was the great fortified city of Cartagena—the Queen of the Indies.

The gathered wealth of the South Seas was brought first of all to Panama. Then it was transported upon mules and under strong guard of well-armed troops across the rocky passes of the mountainous isthmus, to the fortress of Portobelo, near the mouth of the Chagres River. From Portobelo it was shipped to Cartagena, within whose huge walls, defended by ample fortifications, it was believed to be safe from all assault.

At Cartagena the great money-fleets were made up, and, under convoy of large, well-armed war-vessels, sailed for Spain.

Cartagena, well chosen for defense, was an island, connected with the mainland only by fortified bridges and causeways. Before it lay an inner harbor so ample that all the fleets of Spain could easily have found anchorage there. Beyond this harbor was an outer harbor, and between them was a narrow pass of water called the Boca Chica—a slender, snakelike channel through which the tide ran in and out with a torrential rapidity. This pass was defended by two fortresses of stone built according to the best plans of fortification of the day. The outer harbor was connected with the open sea by a wider pass called the Boca Grande, the channel of which was commanded by a fortress as strong as the fortresses of the Boca Chica. The town itself was heavily walled with massive stone masonry.

So Cartagena was thought to be invincible to assault, and the Spanish treasure poured into its vaults for safety.

Then came the war between France and Spain, and the year of grace 1697.

At that time the buccaneers of Hispaniola and Tortuga were at the height of their power. They had had great leaders and great success under those leaders. They had long since lost their original and distinctive characteristic of cattle-killers, and now, after two or three decades of piracy, had come to be very expert at that other trade in which money was to be obtained more easily and in greater abundance than by shooting wild cattle and drying their flesh.

The buccaneer was a picturesque fellow. He belonged to no country and recognized no relationship with any human nationality. He spent his money like a prince, and was very satisfied to live rapidly, even if in so doing his death should come upon him with equal speed. He clothed himself in a picturesque medley of rags and finery. He loved gold and silver ornaments—earrings, finger-rings, bracelets, chains—and he ornamented himself profusely with such things. He wore a great deal of finery of a sort—a tattered shirt or even a bare skin mattered not very much to him provided he was able to hide his seminakedness beneath some such garment as a velvet cloak or a sash of scarlet silk. Patched breeches were not important when he had a fine leather belt with a silver buckle and a good sword hanging to it. And always there were a long-barreled pistol or two and a good handy knife stuck in a waist-belt with which to command respect.

Such was the buccaneer of the seventeenth century.

In the latter part of the year 1696—perhaps about the Christmas season—it began to be rumored among the buccaneers of Hispaniola that a great expedition was about to be undertaken by private French interests and with the knowledge of the French government, against one of the principal Spanish treasure-towns. It was not said just what town was to be attacked, but it was thought to be Santo Domingo.

Gradually the rumor became a fact, and it was known that the commander or general of the expedition was to be M. le Baron de Pointis, an officer high in the French marine service. M. de Pointis was to come with a large fleet from France and the command of a small army of adventurers, with a sprinkling of regular troops.

Then came a call from M. de Casse, the governor of Hispaniola, for volunteers for the expedition.

One can imagine the hubbub that followed among the buccaneers and the colonists. It was a new experience to go pirating in an expedition under sanction of the law. So recruits poured in, and were enrolled as fast as they arrived. And it was not under the name of buccaneers they enlisted. Henceforth they were called filibusters—for, after all, there is a great deal in a name.

So came March in the year 1697, and one day the fleet of M. de Pointis approached the Cape of François and dropped anchor, and he and M. de Casse met together to discuss ways and means.

At first the filibusters were on the lookout for their general from France, but when they met him they were not pleased with him. They were used to a captain who would slap one upon the back and who was not above taking a drink with them upon occasion. M. de Pointis was a very different sort from this; he was proud and haughty and distant, and barely civil. And all the officers and all the gentlemen adventurers that he brought with him from France were equally unsocial in their habits.

So from the very beginning there quickly grew to be two distinct parties in the expedition: the filibusters, who blustered noisily, swore a great deal, and drank without limit; and the officers and adventurers, who ignored the filibusters.

However, thanks perhaps to M. de Casse, terms of agreement were drawn up and signed by the governor and the general. By virtue of this paper the filibusters were to share equally in the profits of the expedition with the French adventurers—a tenth part of the first million and the thirtieth part of the succeeding millions going to those actively engaged in the undertaking, the balance going to the patrons of the expedition at home. Then, all being arranged, they went aboard, hoisted anchor, and set sail, laying their course for the southwest. And then it was known that Cartagena was the objective of the expedition—Cartagena, the invincible fortress, the Queen of the West Indies!

The fleet arrived off Cartagena on the thirteenth of April; on the fifteenth the filibusters were tumbled ashore through a heavy surf that capsized many of the boats and nearly drowned some of the adventurers.

They were then set to capture a high hill that stood a mile or so to the east of the city. On this mount, five or six hundred feet high, stood the fine Church of Nuestra Señora de la Poupa, and this elevation overlooked the avenues and approaches of the land side of the city. The object of seizing this advantageous position was to prevent the resupplying of the city, and to prevent the inhabitants from carrying away any of the treasure gathered.

This was supposed to be the most dangerous and difficult part of the expedition, and the filibusters were quite upset that M. de Pointis should have laid the entire burden of peril upon them so as to save his own men. However, the filibusters went about their work with their usual dash—and, after all, the danger amounted to nothing, for they took the hill handily enough upon the seventeenth, and without the loss of a single man.

Meanwhile, the fleet sailed around into the harbor, passed the defenses of the Boca Grande, and began bombarding the forts of the Boca Chica. Here the Spaniards defended themselves only for a single day. On the sixteenth they surrendered, and the fleet sailed into the inner harbor.

On the third of May the "invincible" city of Cartagena, the Queen of the West Indies, the glory of Spain in the Western World, surrendered after a siege of only eighteen days, and apparently with little or no loss upon either side. The conditions of surrender were as follows:

1. That all public effects and office accounts should be delivered to the captors.

2. That merchants should produce their books and deliver up all money and effects held by them for their customers.

3. That every inhabitant should be free to leave the city or to remain, as he chose; and those who left should first give up all their property to the captors; that those who remained should declare, under penalty of entire confiscation, all the gold, silver, and jewels in their possession; that one-half of this property so declared should be given up to the French, but that the other half should remain in the possession of the owners, and that thereafter they should be protected as subjects of France.

In the face of such conditions one feels sorry for the poor inhabitants of Cartagena, but, at the same time, there is an element of the grotesque in the idea that the well-supplied, strongly walled, and thoroughly fortified city should have surrendered after a siege of only eighteen days to a rag-tag army of cattle-hunters, colonists, needy adventurers, and a scattered handful of regular troops such as M. de Pointis commanded.

M. de Pointis began the important business of collecting his tribute. In the first place he assembled the superiors of the convents and religious houses, telling them that churches and church property would be respected, but that they must give up all money in their possession. Next he appointed M. de Casse as governor of the city to keep order while he did his work. Third, he served notice that, upon pain of death, no filibuster or soldier should enter any house for the purpose of private thievery. Finally he proclaimed that all buried treasure should be confiscated in full, and that anyone who would give information leading to the discovery of such treasure should have a tenth part of it as a reward.

The result of this last proclamation was immediate. "The hope," says the records of the affair, "of receiving a part, with the fear of bad neighbors and false friends, induced the inhabitants to be exceedingly forward in disclosing their riches, and Talleul, who was charged with receiving the treasure, was not able to weigh the gold and silver fast enough."

It was all done in a very businesslike fashion. As the golden harvest poured in, the treasure was packed in boxes, sealed, and sent aboard the men-of-war of the fleet—and no one knew how much was being gathered but M. de Pointis and Talleul.

For a while the filibusters looked on, apparently without knowing exactly what was happening; then they began to wonder how much of this treasure, being packed so snugly on board the men-of-war, would ever find its way back again into their pockets. After a while they began to grumble; then they began to growl; then they began to roar aloud with rage. But M. de Pointis was master of the situation.

After a while M. de Casse himself awoke to the problem. He went to M. de Pointis, and asked, upon behalf of the filibusters, for some statement of the amount that was being collected. The general received him very coolly. At this, as might be expected, loud and angry words passed back and forth between the governor and the general. At the end, M. de Casse withdrew in a huff and went off and shut himself up in a house in the suburbs. He could not very well have followed any plan that would better have fitted the wishes of M. de Pointis. From then on the general collected his treasure in great amounts each time—at a great rate and without interference from anybody.

One can imagine the feelings of the filibusters at beholding their golden opportunity melting away before their very eyes. Nothing remained but to take a hand in the business themselves. Singly at first, then in groups of two or three, then in parties of a dozen or more, they began a systematic looting of whatever M. de Pointis had left, or had not yet taken. The inhabitants, terrified by the danger that menaced them, came to M. de Pointis, asking for protection, but he was powerless to give them aid. We read in the records of this affair that the inhabitants actually resorted to hiring some of the filibusters themselves to defend houses and property against others of their own company.

Meantime this new phase of the situation seriously interfered with M. de Pointis's business of collection, and he set out to find some way of ending the problem.

Suddenly there came a report that ten thousand Indians were approaching the town from the mainland under Spanish leadership, with the intention of lifting the siege. The filibusters were ordered out to meet them, being better used to trailing in the tropical forest than the French adventurers.

They were gone for three or four days; but they did not see a single Indian. Then they marched back again to Cartagena, to find the gates of the city shut against them and well guarded by the few regular troops of the expedition and by cannon from the fleet.

So they sat down outside the gates for fifteen days, cursing, swearing, and kicking their heels. Meanwhile M. de Pointis went on with his business of gathering his golden harvest in peace and quietness. Day after day, chests and boxes of gold and silver treasure went on board the war-vessels and were stowed away in safety, and the filibusters saw it all, roaring with powerless anger. At one time there was some question among them of attempting an attack upon the flagship (the *Scepter*, of eighty-four guns), with the intention of reimbursing themselves from the treasure that had been taken aboard her. But they thought better of that adventure when cooler considerations came to them. So they were obliged to content themselves with sitting outside the gates and swearing a vengeance which they had no means of executing.

By the twenty-fifth of May M. de Pointis's business was finished, and orders were given to embark with as little delay as possible; for news had come that a Dutch and English fleet was approaching. Further orders were issued to the filibusters that they should embark in their own vessels and be sure and stay with the rest of the fleet—if they could.

At this point M. de Casse sent two of his principal officers to the general to demand that he make a statement of the share of the booty that was to come to the filibusters. But by this time M. de Pointis had gone aboard the *Scepter*, where he was safe, and from there he sent word to the officers of the governor that he was ill and could not see them, but that the share of the booty due to the governor and the filibusters was forty thousand crowns, and that he sent his compliments to M. de Casse, and hoped that he would be well satisfied with the result.

That night the French fleet sailed away, and the filibusters were left to shift for themselves, raging at being robbed of their fair share of the adventure.

M. de Casse advised patience, and said that as soon as possible he would take the matter to the French Admiralty Courts. This advice, however, does not seem to have been at all acceptable to the filibusters, who, perhaps, had no great appetite for a taste of the law. So they suggested a better plan—that they reenter Cartagena and squeeze from it what M. de Pointis had left.

M. de Casse, who was, after all, a royal governor, rejected any such plan, but the matter was now no longer in his own control, for the filibusters, since M. de Pointis had left, were masters of the situation. So, on the first of June, M. de Casse sailed away to Hispaniola, and the filibusters were left to shift for themselves.

There they were in front of Cartagena, hardly the better for their adventure, but with the town still left from which to help themselves.

So the filibusters returned to the city, which was now entirely at their mercy without even the dim shadow of M. de Casse's authority as a protection. What followed need not be written in full; what they did may better be imagined than told. It is not said how long they remained, but it was long enough to hunt every corner for remnants of treasure that had been left behind. It is said that they even dug up the graves in their search. In the end, hearing further news of the approach of the Dutch and English fleet, they demanded a payment of five million French livres as the price of their departure without burning the town—and, incredible as it may sound, they got their price.

Then came news, brought by a messenger boat, that the flagship of the Dutch-English fleet was in sight. Immediately the filibusters pulled up anchor and sailed off, scattering as best they could. The war-vessels pursued them; some of the filibuster ships were captured, and some were sunk, but the greater part of them escaped in safety to Hispaniola.

So fell Cartagena, the Pride of the Indies, and it never rose again even as a shadow of its one-time glory. The pride and power of Spain had already crumbled, and with them had crumbled the pride and power of their colonies. As the years passed, in the place of that old-time life that once marched in imitation of splendid Spain through its narrow streets, there came to dwell a population powerless to lift itself above the lowermost level of civilization and progress; instead of storehouses and treasure-houses filled with merchandise and rich with silver and gold, there remained only empty walls and hollow vaults. The filibusters delivered the last thrust that flung Cartagena headlong to the ground to crumble into fragments that shall never again be filled with the glory of its former life.

So fell the treasure-town of Spain in the West Indies.

The Ghost of
Captain Brand

I t is not so easy to tell why shame should be cast upon a man because of something that his grandfather may have done wrong, but the world, which is never overnice in choosing where to lay blame, is often pleased to make the innocent suffer in the place of the guilty.

Barnaby True was a good, honest lad, as young men go, but yet he was never allowed to forget that his grandfather had been that very famous pirate, Captain William Brand, who, after so many marvelous adventures (if one may believe the popular stories and ballads written about him), was murdered in Jamaica by Captain John Malyoe, the commander of his own ship, the *Adventure* galley.

It has never been denied that up to the time of Captain Brand's being commissioned to fight against the South Seas pirates, he had always been respected as an honest and reputable sea-captain.

When he started out upon that adventure it was with a ship, the *Royal Sovereign*, fitted out by some of the most decent merchants of New York. The governor himself had approved of the adventure, and had himself signed Captain Brand's commission. So, if the unfortunate man went astray, he must have had great temptation to do so, many others behaving no better when the opportunity offered in those faraway seas where so many treasures might very easily be taken and no one the wiser.

Stories and ballads described this captain as a most wicked wretch; and if he were, why, he surely suffered and paid for it, for he laid his bones in Jamaica, and never saw his home or his wife and daughter again after he had sailed away on the *Royal Sovereign* on that long, unfortunate voyage, leaving them in New York to the care of strangers.

At the time when he met his fate in Port Royal Harbor, he had two vessels under his command—the *Royal Sovereign*, which was the boat fitted out for him in New York, and the *Adventure* galley, which he was said to have taken somewhere in the South Seas. With these he remained in those waters of Jamaica for over a month after his return from the coasts of Africa, waiting for news from home, which, when it came, was very bad; for the colonial authorities were at that time stirred up against him, and wished to capture him and hang him for piracy, to remove all evidence of their own involvement with such a fellow. So maybe it seemed better to Captain Brand to hide his ill-gotten treasure there in those faraway parts, and afterward to try to bargain with it for his life when he should reach New York, rather than to sail straight for the Americas with what he had earned by his piracies, and so risk losing both life and money.

However that might be, the story was that Captain Brand and his gunner, and Captain Malyoe of the *Adventure* and the sailing master of the *Adventure* all went ashore together with a chest of money (none of them choosing to trust the other three in such an affair), and buried the treasure somewhere on the beach of Port Royal Harbor. The story then has it that they began quarreling about a future division of the money, and that, as a wind-up to the affair, Captain Malyoe shot Captain Brand through the head, while the sailing master of the *Adventure* killed the gunner of the *Royal Sovereign* after the same fashion through the body, and that the murderers then went away, leaving the two stretched out in their own blood on the sand in the staring sun, with no one to know where the money was hidden but the two who had murdered their comrades.

It is a great pity that anyone should have a grandfather who ended his days in such a way as this, but it was no fault of Barnaby True's, nor could he have done anything to prevent it, since he was not even born at the time that his grandfather turned pirate, and was only one year old when the captain met his tragic end. Nevertheless, the boys with whom he went to school never tired of calling him "Pirate" and would sometimes sing for his benefit that famous song beginning thus:

> Oh, my name was Captain Brand,
>   A-sailing,
>   And a-sailing;
> Oh, my name was Captain Brand,
>   A-sailing free.
> Oh, my name was Captain Brand,
> And I sinned by sea and land,
> For I broke God's just command,
>   A-sailing free.

They began quarreling about a future division
of money, and Captain Malyoe shot Captain Brand.

'Twas a vile thing to sing to the grandson of so misfortunate a man, and often little Barnaby True would double up his fists and fight his tormentors at great odds. Sometimes he would go home with a bloody nose to have his poor mother cry over him.

Not that his days were all of teasing and torment: for if his comrades did treat him so, why, then, there were other times when he and they were as great friends as could be, and would go in swimming together where there was a bit of sandy land along the East River above Fort George. Or, maybe the very next day after he had fought with the other fellows, he would go rambling with them up the Bowerie Road, perhaps to help them steal cherries from some old Dutch farmer, forgetting during such an adventure what a thief his own grandfather had been.

Well, when Barnaby True was between sixteen and seventeen years old he was taken into employment in the counting-house of Mr. Roger Hartright, the well-known West Indies merchant, and Barnaby's own stepfather.

It was the kindness of this good man that not only found a place for Barnaby in the counting-house, but advanced him so fast that by the time Barnaby was twenty-one years old he had made four voyages as commerce officer to the West Indies in Mr. Hartright's ship, the *Belle Helen*. Soon after he was twenty-one he undertook a fifth. Nor was it in any minor position as mere commerce officer that he acted, but rather as the personal agent of Mr. Hartright, who, having no children of his own, was eager to advance Barnaby into a position of trust and responsibility in the counting-house, as though he were indeed a son, so that even the captain of the ship had little more respect aboard than Barnaby, young as he was in years.

As for the agents and customers of Mr. Hartright throughout these parts, they also, knowing how the good man had adopted his interests, were very polite and obliging to Barnaby. This was especially true of Mr. Ambrose Greenfield, of Kingston, Jamaica, who during Barnaby's visits to those parts did all that he could to make his stay in that town agreeable and pleasant.

Such was the history of Barnaby True to the time of the beginning of this story, without which you shall hardly be able to understand the reason for the most extraordinary adventures that befell him shortly after he turned twenty-one, nor the logic of their results after they had occurred.

It was during Barnaby's fifth voyage to the West Indies that the first of those extraordinary adventures happened. At that time the young man had been in Kingston for the best part of four weeks, lodging at the house of a respectable widow, Mrs. Anne Bolles, who, with three pleasant and agreeable daughters, kept a clean and well-served lodging house on the outskirts of the town.

One morning, as Barnaby sat—clad only in loose cotton pants, a shirt, and a jacket, and with slippers upon his feet, as is the custom in that country, where everyone tries to keep as cool as may be— while he sat thus, sipping his coffee, Eliza, the youngest of the three daughters, came and gave him a note, which, she said, a stranger had just handed to her at the door, going away again without waiting for a reply. You may guess Barnaby's surprise when he opened the note and read as follows:

Mr. Barnaby True

Sir: Though you don't know me, I know you, and I tell you this: if you will be at Pratt's Tavern on Harbor Street on Friday next at eight o'clock in the evening, and will accompany the man who shall say to you, "The *Royal Sovereign* has come in," you shall learn something the most to your advantage that ever befell you. Sir, keep this note, and show it to him who shall address these words to you, to certify that you are the man he seeks.

Such was the wording of the note, which was without an address, and without any signature whatever.

The first emotion that stirred Barnaby was one of extreme amazement. Then the thought came into his mind that some witty fellow, of whom he knew a good many in that town—and wild pranksters they were—was attempting to play some clever joke upon him. But all that Eliza could tell him when he questioned her concerning the messenger was that the bearer of the note was a tall, stout man, with a red kerchief around his neck and copper buckles on his shoes, and that he had the appearance of a sailor, having a long, thick braid hanging down his back. But what was such a description as that in a busy seaport town, full of scores of men to fit such a description. Barnaby put the note in his wallet, determining to show it to his good friend Mr. Greenfield that evening, and to ask his advice about it. So he did show it, and that gentleman's opinion was the same as his—that some fellow wished to play a prank on him, and that the letter was of no importance.

Nevertheless, though Barnaby was now convinced that his opinion about the letter was correct, he still decided that he would see the business through to the end, and would be at Pratt's Tavern, as the note demanded, on the day and at the time specified.

Pratt's Tavern was at that time a very fine and well-known place of its sort, with good tobacco and rum, and with a garden behind it that, sloping down to the harborfront, was planted densely with palms and ferns grouped into clusters with flowers and plants. There were a number of little tables, with red and blue and white paper lanterns hung among the greenery, where gentlemen and ladies used sometimes to go in the evening to sit and drink lime juice and sugar and water (and sometimes a taste of something stronger), and to look out across the water at the ships in the cool of the night.

To there Barnaby went, a little before the time requested in the

note, and, passing directly through the tavern and the garden beyond, chose a table at the lower end of the garden close to the
water's edge, where he would not be easily seen by anyone coming
into the place. Then, ordering some grog and a pipe of tobacco, he
watched for the appearance of those witty fellows whom he suspected would presently come to see the end of their prank and to
enjoy his confusion.

The spot was pleasant enough; for the land breeze, blowing
strong and full, set the leaves of the palm tree above his head to
rattling and clattering continually against the sky, where, the moon
then being about full, they shone every now and then like blades of
steel. The waves also were splashing against the little landing place
at the foot of the garden, sounding very cool in the night, and
sparkling all over the harbor where the moon caught the edges of
the water. A great many vessels were lying at anchor, with the dark
form of a man-of-war looming up above them in the moonlight.

There Barnaby sat for the best part of an hour, smoking his pipe
and sipping his grog, and seeing not so much as a single thing that
might concern the note he had received.

It was not far from half an hour after the time appointed in the
note when a rowboat came suddenly out of the night and pulled up
to the landing place at the foot of the garden, and three or four
men came ashore in the darkness. Without saying a word among
themselves they chose a nearby table and, sitting down, ordered
rum and water, and began drinking in silence. They might have sat
there about five minutes when Barnaby True became aware that
they were observing him very curiously. Then, almost immediately,
one, who was plainly the leader of the party, called out to him,
"How now, messmate! Won't you come and drink a bit of rum
with us?"

"Why, no," said Barnaby, answering very civilly. "I have drunk
enough already, and more would only heat my blood."

The Fate of a Treasure-Town

The Ghost of Captain Brand

"All the same," replied the stranger, "I think you will come and drink with us; for, unless I am mistaken, you are Mr. Barnaby True, and I am come here to tell you that the *Royal Sovereign* has come in."

Barnaby True was never more surprised in all his life than he was at hearing these words uttered in so unexpected a manner. He had been expecting to hear them under such different circumstances that, now that his ears heard them addressed to him, and so seriously, by a perfect stranger, who, with others, had mysteriously come ashore out of the darkness, he could scarce believe that his ears heard correctly. His heart suddenly began beating at a tremendous rate. Had he been an older and wiser man, he probably would have declined the adventure, instead of leaping blindly, as he did, into that of which he could see neither the beginning nor the ending. But being barely one-and-twenty years of age, and having an adventurous disposition that would have carried him into almost anything that had a smack of uncertainty or danger about it, he said, in a pretty easy tone (though who knows how it was put on for the occasion): "Well, then, if that is so, and if the *Royal Sovereign* has indeed come in, why, I'll join you, since you are so kind as to ask me." And he went across to the other table, carrying his pipe with him, and sat down, with all the appearance of ease he could assume upon the occasion.

"Well, Mr. Barnaby True," said the man who had addressed him before, as soon as Barnaby had settled himself, speaking in a low tone of voice, so there would be no danger of any others hearing the words—"Well, Mr. Barnaby True—for I shall call you by your name, to show you that though I know you, you don't know me—I am glad to see that you are man enough to enter into this affair, though you can't see to the bottom of it. For it shows me that you are a man of courage, and are deserving of the fortune that is to befall you tonight. Nevertheless, first of all, I must ask that you show me a piece of paper that you have with you before we go a step farther."

"Very well," said Barnaby. "I have it here safe and sound, and see it you shall." And without more ado he pulled out his wallet, opened it, and handed the other the mysterious note he had received the day or two before. Then the stranger, drawing the candle to him, immediately began reading it.

This gave Barnaby True a moment or two to look at him. He was a tall, stout man, with a red handkerchief tied around his neck, and with copper buckles on his shoes, so that Barnaby could only wonder whether he was not the very same man who had given the note to Eliza Bolles at the door of his lodging-house.

" 'Tis all right and straight as it should be," the other said, after he had glanced over the note. "And now that the paper is read" (suiting his action to his words), "I'll just burn it, for safety's sake."

And so he did, twisting it up and setting it to the flame of the candle.

"And now," he said, continuing, "I'll tell you what I am here for. I was sent to ask you if you're man enough to take your life in your own hands and to go with me in that boat down there. Say yes, and we'll start without wasting more time, for the Devil is ashore here at Jamaica—though you don't know what that means—and if he gets ahead of us, why, then we may whistle for what we are after. Say no, and I go away again, and I promise that you shall never be troubled again in this way. So now speak up plain, young gentleman, and tell us what is your mind in this business, and whether you will adventure any farther or not."

If Barnaby hesitated it was not for long. It cannot be said that his courage did not waver for a moment; but if it did, it was not for long, and when he spoke up it was with a voice as steady as could be.

"To be sure, I'm man enough to go with you," he said, "and if you mean me any harm I can look out for myself; and if I can't, why, here is something that can look out for me," and he lifted up the flap of his coat pocket and showed the butt of a pistol he had brought with him when he had set out from his lodging-house that evening.

At this, the other man burst out laughing. "Come," said he, "you indeed have courage, and I like your spirit. All the same, no one in all the world means you less ill will than I, and so, if you have to use that pistol, 'twill not be upon us who are your friends, but only upon one who is more wicked than the Devil himself. So come, and let us get away."

Then he and the others, who had not spoken a single word during all this time, rose from the table; and he having paid the bills for all, they all went down together to the boat that still lay at the landing place at the bottom of the garden.

Barnaby could see that it was a large yawl manned with ten men to row, and there were two lanterns and three or four iron shovels.

The man who had conducted the conversation with Barnaby True, and who was plainly the captain of the party, stepped immediately down into the boat; Barnaby followed, and the others followed after him. The instant they were seated the boat was shoved off and the rowers began pulling straight out into the harbor, and then, at some distance away, under the stern of the man-of-war.

Not a word was spoken after they had left the shore; they might all have been ghosts, to judge by the silence of the party. Barnaby True was too full of his own thoughts to talk—and serious enough thoughts they were by this time, with enlistment agents to lure a man at every turn, and press-gangs to carry a man off so that he might never be heard of again. As for the others, they did not seem to choose to say anything now that they had him fully involved with their adventure.

And so the crew pulled on in perfect silence for the best part of
an hour, the leader of the expedition directing the course of the
boat straight across the harbor, as though toward the mouth of the
Rio Cobra River. Indeed, this was their destination, as Barnaby
could after a while see, by the low point of land with a great long
row of coconut palms upon it (the appearance of which he knew
very well), which soon began to loom up out of the milky dimness
of the moonlight. As they approached the river, they found the tide
was running strongly out of it, so that some distance away from the
stream it gurgled and rippled alongside the boat as the rowing crew
pulled strongly against it. Thus they came up under what was either a point of land or an islet covered with a thick growth of
mangrove trees. But still no one spoke a single word as to their
destination or what their business was.

The night, now that they were close to the shore, was loud with
the noise of running tidewater, and the air was heavy with the
smell of mud and marsh, and over all was the whiteness of the
moonlight, with a few stars pricking out here and there in the sky.
Everything was so strange and silent and mysterious that Barnaby
could not free himself of the feeling that it was all a dream.

So, the rowers bending to the oars, the boat came slowly around
from under the clump of mangrove bushes and out into the open
water again.

At the moment it did so, the leader of the expedition called out
in a sharp voice, and the men instantly lay on their oars.

Almost at the same instant Barnaby True became aware that
there was another boat coming down the river toward where they
lay, now drifting with the strong tide out into the harbor again, and
he knew that it was because of the approach of that boat that the
other had called upon his men to cease rowing.

The other boat, as well as he could see in the distance, was full of
men, some of whom appeared to be armed, for even in the darkness

the shine of the moonlight glimmered sharply now and then on the barrels of muskets or pistols. In the silence that followed after their own rowing had ceased Barnaby True could hear the *chug! chug!* of the oars sounding louder and louder through the watery stillness of the night as the boat drew nearer and nearer. But he knew nothing of what it all meant, nor whether these others were friends or enemies, or what was to happen next.

The oarsmen of the approaching boat did not for a moment stop their rowing, not till they had come pretty close to Barnaby and his companions. Then a man who sat in the stern ordered them to cease rowing, and as they lay on their oars he stood up. As they passed, Barnaby True could see him plainly, the moonlight shining fully upon him—a large, stout gentleman with a round red face, and clad in a fine lace-bordered coat of red cloth. Amidship of the boat was a box or chest about the size of a middle-sized traveling trunk, but covered with cakes of sand and dirt. In the act of passing, the gentleman, still standing, pointed at it with an elegant gold-headed cane which he held in his hand. "Have you come after this, Abraham Dawling?" said he, and then his countenance broke into as evil, malignant a grin as ever Barnaby True saw in all of his life.

The other did not immediately reply with so much as a single word, but sat as still as any stone. Then, at last, the other boat having gone by, he suddenly appeared to regain his wits, for he bawled out after it, "Very well, Jack Malyoe! Very well, Jack Malyoe! You've got ahead of us this time again, but next time is the third, and then it shall be our turn, even if William Brand must come back from hell to settle with you."

This he shouted out as the other boat passed farther and farther away, but to it the fine gentleman made no reply except to burst out into a great roaring fit of laughter.

There was another man among the armed men in the stern of the passing boat—a villainous, lean man with lantern jaws, and the top of his head as bald as the palm of a hand. As the boat went away into the night with the tide and the headway the oars had given it, he grinned so that the moonlight shone white on his big teeth. Then, flourishing a great big pistol, he said—and Barnaby could hear every word he spoke—"Do but give me the word, Your Honor, and I'll put another bullet through the son of a sea cook."

But the gentleman said some words to forbid him, and with that the boat was gone into the night. Presently Barnaby could hear that the men at the oars had begun rowing again, leaving them lying there, without a single word being said for a long time.

Soon one of those in Barnaby's boat spoke up. "Where shall you go now?" he said.

At this the leader of the expedition appeared suddenly to come back to himself, and to find his voice again. "Go?" he roared out. "Go to the Devil! Go? Go where you choose! Go? Go back again— that's where we'll go!" and he then began cursing and swearing until he foamed at the lips, as though he had gone crazy, while the crew began rowing back across the harbor as fast as they could lay oars into the water.

They put Barnaby True ashore below the old customhouse; but so bewildered and shaken was he by all that had happened, and by what he had seen, and by the names that he heard spoken, that he was scarcely conscious of any of the familiar things among which he found himself thus standing. And so he walked up the moonlit street toward his lodging like one drunk or bewildered; for John Malyoe was the name of the captain of the *Adventure* galley—he who had shot Barnaby's own grandfather—and Abraham Dawling was the name of the gunner of the *Royal Sovereign* who had been shot at the same time with the pirate captain, and who, with him, had been left stretched out in the staring sun by the murderers.

The whole business had taken hardly two hours, but it was as though that time was no part of Barnaby's life, but all a part of some other life, so dark and strange and mysterious that it in no way belonged to him.

As for that box covered with mud, he could only guess what it contained and what the finding of it signified.

But of this Barnaby said nothing to anyone, nor did he tell a single living soul what he had seen that night. But he nursed it in his own mind, where it lay so big for a while that he could think of little or nothing else for days after.

Mr. Greenfield, Mr. Hartright's agent in these parts, lived in a fine brick house just out of the town, on the Mona Road. His family consisted of a wife and two daughters—brisk, lively young ladies with black hair and eyes, and very fine bright teeth that shone whenever they laughed, and with plenty to say for themselves. Barnaby True was often asked to this house for a family dinner. Indeed, it was a pleasant home to visit, and to sit upon the veranda with the good old gentleman and look out toward the mountains, while the young ladies laughed and talked, or played upon the guitar and sang. And often it was strongly upon Barnaby's mind to speak to the good gentleman and tell him what he had beheld that night out in the harbor. But always he would think better of it and hold his peace, falling to thinking, as the old gentlemen smoked away upon their cigars.

A day or two before the *Belle Helen* sailed from Kingston, Mr. Greenfield stopped Barnaby True as he was going through the office to ask him to come to dinner that night (for there within the tropics they breakfast at eleven o'clock and take dinner in the cool of the evening, because of the heat, and not at midday, as is done in more temperate latitudes). "I would have you meet," says Mr. Greenfield, "your chief passenger for New York, and his granddaughter, for whom the state cabin and the two staterooms are to be fitted as here ordered [showing a letter]—Sir John Malyoe and Miss Marjorie Malyoe. Did you ever hear tell of Captain Jack Malyoe, Master Barnaby?"

Now I do believe that Mr. Greenfield had no notion at all that old Captain Brand was Barnaby True's own grandfather and Captain John Malyoe his murderer, but when he so thrust at him the name of that man, what with that in itself and the adventure through which he himself had just passed, and with his brooding upon it until it was so large in his mind, it was like hitting him a blow to so fling the questions at him. Nevertheless, he was able to reply, with a pretty straight face, that he had heard of Captain Malyoe and who he was.

"Well," says Mr. Greenfield, "if Jack Malyoe was a desperate pirate and a wild, reckless blade twenty years ago, why, he is Sir John Malyoe now and the owner of a fine estate in Devonshire. Well, Master Barnaby, when one is a baron and come into the inheritance of a fine estate (though I do hear it is vastly weighed down with debts), the world will wink its eye to much that he may have done twenty years ago. I do hear say, though, that his own kin still turn the cold shoulder to him." To this address Barnaby answered nothing.

And so that night Barnaby True came face to face for the first time with the man who murdered his own grandfather—

the greatest beast of a man that ever he met in all of his life.

That time in the harbor he had seen Sir John Malyoe at a distance and in the darkness. Now that he beheld him nearby it seemed to him that he had never looked at a more evil face in all his life. Not that the man was altogether ugly, for he had a good nose and a fine double chin. But his eyes stood out like balls and were red and watery, and he winked them continually, as though they were always smarting; and his lips were thick and purple-red, and his fat, red cheeks were marked here and there with little purple veins; and when he spoke his voice rattled so in his throat that it made one wish to clear one's own throat to listen to him. So, what with a pair of fat, white hands, and that hoarse voice, and his swollen face, and his thick lips sticking out, it seemed to Barnaby True he had never seen a face so distasteful to him as that one into which he then looked.

But if Sir John Malyoe was so displeasing to Barnaby's taste, why, the granddaughter, even this first time he beheld her, seemed to him to be the most beautiful, lovely young lady that ever he saw. She had a thin, fair skin, red lips, and yellow hair—though it was then powdered pretty white for the occasion—and the bluest eyes that Barnaby beheld in all of his life. A sweet, timid creature, who seemed not to dare so much as to speak a word for herself without looking to Sir John for permission to do so and who would shrink and shudder whenever he would suddenly speak to her or direct a quick glance at her. When she did speak, it was in so low a voice that Barnaby had to bend his head to hear her, and even if she smiled she would catch herself and look up as though to see if she had permission to be cheerful.

As for Sir John, he sat at dinner like a pig, and gobbled and ate and drank, smacking his lips all the while, but with hardly a word to either her or Mrs. Greenfield or to Barnaby True, and with a sour, sullen air, as though he would say, "Your food and drink are no better than they should be, but I must eat 'em or nothing." A great bloated beast of a man!

Only after dinner was over and the young lady and the two misses sat off in a corner together did Barnaby hear her talk with any ease. Then, to be sure, her tongue became loose, and she prattled away at a great rate, though hardly above her breath, until suddenly her grandfather called out, in his hoarse, rattling voice, that it was time to go. At this, she stopped short in what she was saying and jumped up from her chair, looking as frightened as though she had been caught in something wrong and was to be punished for it.

Barnaby True and Mr. Greenfield both went out to see the two into their coach, where Sir John's man stood holding the lantern. And who should he be, to be sure, but that same lean villain with bald head who had offered to shoot the leader of Barnaby's expedition out on the harbor that night! One of the circles of light from the lantern shone up into his face, and Barnaby True knew him the moment he laid eyes upon him. Though he could not have recognized the young man, he grinned at him in the most impudent, familiar fashion, and never so much as touched his hat either to him or to Mr. Greenfield. But as soon as his master and his young mistress had entered the coach, he banged to the door and scrambled up on the seat alongside the driver, and so drove away—without a word, but with another impudent grin, this time favoring both Barnaby and the old gentleman.

The next day Sir John Malyoe's belongings began to come aboard the *Belle Helen,* and in the afternoon that same lean, villainous manservant came skipping across the gangplank as nimble as a goat, with two men behind him lugging a great sea chest. "What!" he cried out. "And so you is the supercargo, is you? Why, I thought you was more account when I saw you last night sitting talking with His Honor like his equal. Well, no matter; 'tis something to have a brisk, genteel young fellow for a commerce officer. So come, my hearty, lend a hand, will you, and help me set His Honor's cabin to rights."

What a speech this was to endure from such a fellow! And Barnaby so high in his own esteem, and holding himself a gentleman! Well, what with his distaste for the villain, and what with such odious familiarity, you can guess into what temper so bold an address must have cast him. "You'll find the steward yonder," he said, "and he'll show you the cabin," and he turned and walked away with dignity, leaving the other standing where he was.

As Barnaby entered his own cabin he could see, out of the corner of his eye, that the fellow was still standing where he had left him, regarding him with a most evil, malevolent expression, so he had the satisfaction of knowing that he had made one enemy during that voyage who was not very likely to forgive or forget what he must regard as a slight.

The next day Sir John Malyoe himself came aboard, accompanied by his granddaughter, and followed by this man, who was followed by four more men, who carried among them two trunks, not large in size, but very heavy in weight, and toward which Sir John and his follower devoted the utmost care to see that they were properly carried into the cabin he was to occupy. Barnaby True was standing in the great cabin as they passed close by him. But though Sir John Malyoe looked hard at him and straight in the face, he never so much as spoke a single word, or showed by a look or a sign that he knew who Barnaby was. At this the serving man, who saw it all with eyes as quick as a cat's, fell to grinning and chuckling to see Barnaby in his turn so slighted.

The young lady, who also saw it all, flushed red, then in the instant of passing looked straight at Barnaby, and bowed and smiled at him with a most sweet and gracious friendliness, then the next moment recovering herself, as though mightily frightened at what she had done.

The same day the *Belle Helen* sailed, with as beautiful, sweet weather as ever a body could wish for.

There were only two other passengers aboard, the Reverend Simon Styles, the master of a flourishing academy in Spanish Town, and his wife—a good, worthy old couple, but very quiet. They would sit in the great cabin by the hour together reading, so that, what with Sir John Malyoe staying all the time in his own cabin with those two trunks he held so precious, it fell upon Barnaby True in great part to show attention to the young lady; and glad enough he was of the opportunity, as anyone may guess. For when you consider a brisk, lively young man of one-and-twenty and a sweet, beautiful miss of eighteen so thrown together day after day for two weeks, the weather being very fair and the ship tossing and bowling along before a fine humming breeze that sent white caps all over the sea, and with nothing for them to do but sit and look at that blue sea and the bright sky overhead, it is not hard to suppose what was to befall, and what pleasure it was to Barnaby True to show attention to her.

But, oh, those days when a man is young, and, whether wisely or not, fallen in love! How often during that voyage did Barnaby lie awake in his berth at night, tossing this way and that without sleep —not that he wanted to sleep if he could, but he would rather lie so awake thinking about her and staring into the darkness!

Poor fool! He might have known that the end must come to such a fool's paradise before very long. For who was he to look up to Sir John Malyoe's granddaughter—he, the commerce officer of a merchant ship, and she the granddaughter of a baronet?

Nevertheless, things went along very smooth and pleasant, until one evening, when it all came suddenly to an end. At that time Barnaby and the young lady had been standing for a long while together, leaning over the rail and looking out across the water through the dusk toward the west, where the sky was still of a lingering brightness. She had been mightily quiet and dull all that evening, but now she began, without any preface whatever, to tell Barnaby about herself and her affairs. She said that she and her grandfather were going to New York that they might take passage from there to Boston town, there to meet her cousin Captain Malyoe, who was stationed in garrison at that place. Then she went on to say that Captain Malyoe was the next heir to the Devonshire estate, and that she and he were to be married in the fall.

But, poor Barnaby! What a fool was he, to be sure! It is likely that when she first began to speak about Captain Malyoe he knew what was coming. But now that she had told him, he could say nothing, but stood there staring across the ocean, his breath coming hot and dry as ashes in his throat. She, poor thing, went on to say, in a very low voice, that she had liked him from the very first moment she had seen him, and had been very happy for these days, and would always think of him as a dear friend who had been very kind to her, who had so little pleasure in life, and so would always remember him.

Then they were both silent, until at last Barnaby said, though in a hoarse and croaking voice, that Captain Malyoe must be a very happy man, and that if he were in Captain Malyoe's place he would be the happiest man in the world. Then he went on to tell her, with his head all in a whirl, that he, too, loved her, and that what she had told him struck him to the heart, and made him the most miserable, unhappy wretch in the whole world.

She was not angry at what he said, nor did she turn to look at him, but only said, in a low voice, that he should not talk so, for it could only be painful to them both to speak of such things, and that whether she would or not, she must do everything as her grandfather bid her, for he was indeed a terrible man.

To this poor Barnaby could only repeat that he loved her with all his heart, that he had hoped for nothing in his love, but that he was now the most miserable man in the world.

It was at this moment, so tragic for him, that someone who had been hiding near them all the while suddenly moved away, and Barnaby True could see in the darkness that it was that villain manservant of Sir John Malyoe's and knew that he must have overheard all that had been said.

The man went straight to the great cabin, and poor Barnaby, his brain all atingle, stood looking after him, feeling that now indeed the last drop of bitterness had been added to his trouble to have such a wretch overhear what he had said.

The young lady could not have seen the fellow, for she continued leaning over the rail, with Barnaby True standing at her side, not moving, but in such a tumult of passion that he was like one bewildered, his heart beating as though to smother him.

So they stood, for quite a long time when suddenly Sir John Malyoe came running out of the cabin, without his hat, but carrying his gold-headed cane, and went straight across the deck to where Barnaby and the young lady stood, that spying wretch close at his heels, grinning like an imp.

"You hussy!" bawled out Sir John, so soon as he had come pretty near them, in so loud a voice that all on deck might have heard the words. As he spoke he waved his cane back and forth as though he would have struck the young lady, who, shrinking back almost upon the deck, crouched as though to escape such a blow. "You hussy!" he bawled out with vile oaths, too horrible here to be set down. "What are you doing here with this Yankee officer, who is not fit for a gentlewoman to wipe her feet upon? Get to your cabin, before I lay this cane across your shoulders!"

What with the whirling of Barnaby's brains and the passion into which he was already melted, what with his despair and his love, and his anger at this address, a man gone mad could scarcely be less accountable for his actions than was he at that moment. Hardly knowing what he did, he put his hand against Sir John Malyoe's chest and thrust him violently back, yelling at him in a great, loud, hoarse voice for threatening a young lady, and saying that for a farthing he would wrench the stick out of his hand and throw it overboard.

Sir John went staggering back with the push Barnaby gave him, and then caught himself up again. Then he ran roaring at Barnaby, whirling his cane about, and probably would have struck him (and who knows then what might have happened) had not his man-servant caught him and held him back.

"Keep back!" cried out Barnaby, still hoarse. "Keep back! If you strike me with that stick I'll throw you overboard!"

By this time, with all the noise of loud voices and the stamping of feet, some of the crew and others aboard were hurrying up, and the next moment Captain Manly and the first mate, Mr. Freesden, came running out of the cabin. But Barnaby could not now stop himself.

"And who are you, anyhow," he cried out, "to threaten to strike me and to insult me, who is as good as you? You dare not strike me! You may shoot a man from behind, as you shot poor Captain Brand on the Rio Cobra River, but you won't dare strike me face to face. I know who you are and what you are!"

By this time Sir John Malyoe had ceased to endeavor to strike him, but stood stock-still, his great bulging eyes staring as though they would pop out of his head.

"What's all this?" cried Captain Manly, bustling up to them with Mr. Freesden. "What does all this mean?"

But Barnaby was too far gone now to contain himself until all that he had to say was out.

"The wretched villain insulted me and insulted the young lady," he cried out, panting in the extremity of his passion. "Then he threatened to strike me with his cane. But I know who he is and what he is. I know what he's got in his cabin in those two trunks, and where he found it, and to whom it belongs. He found it on the shores of the Rio Cobra River, and I have only to open my mouth and tell what I know about it."

At this Captain Manly clapped his hand upon Barnaby's shoulder and fell to shaking him so that he could scarcely stand, calling out to him the while to be silent. "What do you mean?" he cried. "An officer of this ship to quarrel with a passenger of mine! Go straight to your cabin, and stay there till I give you leave to come out again."

At this Barnaby came somewhat back to himself and into his wits again with a jump. "But he threatened to strike me with his cane, Captain," he cried out, "and that I won't stand from any man!"

"No matter what he did," said Captain Manly, very sternly. "Go to your cabin, as I bid you, and stay there till I tell you to come out again, and when we get to New York I'll take pains to tell your stepfather how you have behaved. I'll have no such rioting as this aboard my ship."

Barnaby True looked around him, but the young lady was gone. Nor, in the blindness of his frenzy, had he seen when she had gone nor where she went. As for Sir John Malyoe, he stood in the light of a lantern, his face as white as ashes, and if a look could kill, the dreadful, malevolent stare he fixed upon Barnaby True would have slain him where he stood.

After Captain Manly had so shaken some wits into poor Barnaby he, unhappy wretch, went to his cabin, as he was told to do. There, after shutting the door and flinging himself down upon his berth, he yielded to an intense feeling of humiliation. There he lay staring into the darkness, until, in spite of his suffering and despair, he dozed off into a light sleep that was more like waking than sleep, being possessed continually by the most vivid and distasteful dreams, from which he would awaken only to doze off and to dream again.

It was from the midst of one of these dreams that he was suddenly aroused by the noise of a pistol shot, and then the noise of another and another, and then a great bump and a grinding jar, and then the sound of many footsteps running across the deck and down into the great cabin. Then came a tremendous uproar of voices in the great cabin, the struggling as of men's bodies being tossed about, striking violently against the partitions and bulkheads. At the same instant arose a screaming of women's voices, and one voice—Sir John Malyoe's—crying out: "You villains! You filthy villains!" And with the sudden detonation of a pistol he fired into the close space of the great cabin.

Barnaby was out in the middle of his cabin in a moment, and taking only time enough to snatch one of the pistols that hung at the head of his berth, flung himself out into the great cabin, to find it as black as night, the lantern slung there having been either blown out or dashed out into darkness. The incredibly dark space was full of uproar, the hubbub and confusion pierced through and through by the sound of women's voices screaming, one in the cabin and the other in the stateroom beyond. Almost immediately Barnaby pitched headlong over two or three struggling men scuffling together upon the deck, falling with a great clatter and the loss of his pistol, which, however, he regained almost immediately.

What all the uproar meant he could not tell, but he presently heard Captain Manly's voice from somewhere suddenly calling out, "You bloody pirate, would you choke me to death?" With that, some notion of what had happened came to him like a flash—that they had been attacked in the night by pirates.

Looking toward the stairway, he saw, outlined against the darkness of the night, the blacker form of a man's figure, standing still and motionless as a statue in the midst of all this hubbub; by some instinct he knew in a moment that that must be the master maker of all this devil's brew. Then, still kneeling upon the deck, he covered the bosom of that shadowy figure pointblank, as he thought, with his pistol, and instantly pulled the trigger.

In the flash of red light, and in the instant, stunning sound of the pistol shot, Barnaby saw, as stamped upon the blackness, a broad, flat face with fishy eyes, a lean, bony forehead with what appeared to be a great blotch of blood upon the side, a cocked hat trimmed with gold lace, a red scarf across the breast, and the gleam of brass buttons. Then the darkness, very thick and black, swallowed everything again.

But in the instant Sir John Malyoe called out, in a great loud voice: " 'Tis William Brand!" And then came the sound of someone falling heavily down.

The next moment Barnaby's sight came back to him again in the darkness. He saw that dark and motionless figure still standing exactly where it had stood before, and so knew either that he had missed it or else that it was of so supernatural a sort that a lead bullet might do it no harm. Though if it was indeed a ghost that Barnaby beheld in that moment, there is this to say: that he saw it as plain as ever he saw a living man in all his life.

This was the last Barnaby knew, for the next moment somebody —whether by accident or design, he never knew—struck him such a terrible, violent blow upon the side of the head that he saw forty thousand stars flash before his eyes; then, with a great humming in his head, he swooned dead away.

When Barnaby True came back to his senses again it was to find himself being cared for with great skill and kindness, his head bathed with cold water, and a bandage being bound around it as carefully as though a surgeon was attending to him.

He could not immediately recall what had happened to him, not until he had opened his eyes to find himself in a strange cabin, extremely well fitted and painted with white and gold, the light of a lantern shining in his eyes, together with the gray of the early daylight through the deadeye. Two men were bending over him— one, a black man in a striped shirt, with a yellow handkerchief around his head and silver earrings in his ears; the other, a white man, clad in a strange, flashy dress of a foreign make, and with a great mustache hanging down, and with gold earrings in his ears.

It was the latter who was attending to Barnaby's injury with such extreme care and gentleness.

All this Barnaby saw with his first clear consciousness after his swoon. Then remembering what had happened to him, and his head beating as though it would split apart, he shut his eyes again, making a great effort to keep himself from groaning aloud, and wondering as to what kind of pirates these could be who would first knock a man in the head and then take such care to fetch him back to life again, and to make him easy and comfortable.

Nor did he open his eyes again, but lay there wondering and gathering his wits together until the bandage was properly tied around his head and sewed together. Then once more he opened his eyes, and he looked up to ask where he was.

Either they who were attending to him did not choose to reply, or else they could not speak English, for they made no answer, except by signs. The white man, seeing that Barnaby was now able to speak, and so had come back into his senses again, nodded his head three or four times, and smiled with a grin of his white teeth, and then pointed, as though toward a saloon beyond. At the same time the black man held up Barnaby's coat and beckoned for him to put it on. Barnaby, seeing that it was required of him to meet someone outside, arose, though with a good deal of effort, and permitted the man to help him on with his coat, still feeling dizzy and uncertain upon his legs, his head beating fit to split, and the vessel rolling and pitching at a great rate.

So, still sick and dizzy, he went out into what was indeed a fine room beyond—the saloon—painted in white and gilt like the cabin he had just left, and furnished in the nicest fashion—a mahogany table, polished very bright, extending the length of the room, and a number of bottles, together with glasses of clear crystal, arranged in a hanging rack above.

Here at the table a man was sitting with his back to Barnaby, clad in a rough pea-jacket, and with a red handkerchief tied around his throat, his feet stretched out before him, and he smoked a pipe of tobacco with all the ease and comfort in the world.

As Barnaby came in the man turned around and, to Barnaby's profound astonishment, presented toward him in the light of the lantern—the dawn shining pretty strong through the skylight—the face of that very man who had conducted the mysterious expedition that night across Kingston Harbor to the Rio Cobra River.

This man looked steadily at Barnaby True for a moment or two, and then burst out laughing; and, indeed, Barnaby, standing there with the bandage about his head, must have looked like a very amusing picture of that astonishment he felt at finding who was this pirate into whose hands he had fallen.

"Well," said the seated man, "and so you be up at last, and no great harm done, I'll be bound. And how does your head feel by now, my young master?"

To this Barnaby made no reply, but seated himself at the table over against the speaker, who pushed a bottle of grog toward him, together with a glass from the swinging shelf above.

He watched Barnaby fill his glass, and as soon as he had done so began immediately by saying: "I do suppose you think you were treated very badly, to be so handled last night. Well, so you were treated badly enough—though who hit you that crack upon the head I know no more than a child unborn. Well, I am sorry for the way you were handled, but there is this much to say, and of that you may believe me: that nothing was meant to you but kindness, and before you are through with us all you will believe that well enough."

Here he helped himself to a taste of grog, and sucking in his lips, went on again with what he had to say. "Do you remember," said he, "that expedition of ours in Kingston Harbor?"

"Why, yes," said Barnaby True, "nor am I likely to forget it."

"And do you remember what I said to that villain, Jack Malyoe, that night as his boat went by us?"

"As to that," said Barnaby True, "I do not know that I can say yes or no, but if you will tell me, I will maybe answer you."

"Why, I mean this," said the pirate. "I said that the villain had got the better of us once again, but that next time it would be our turn, even if William Brand himself had to come back from hell to put the business through."

"I remember something of the sort," said Barnaby, "now that you speak of it, but still I am all in the dark as to what you are driving at."

The pirate looked at him very cunningly for a little while, his head on one side, and his eyes half shut. Then, as if satisfied, he suddenly burst out laughing. "Look here," said he, "and I'll show you something." And with that, moving to one side, he disclosed a couple of traveling cases or small trunks with brass studs, so exactly like those that Sir John Malyoe had fetched aboard at Jamaica that

Barnaby, putting this and that together, knew that they must be the same.

Barnaby had a strong enough suspicion as to what those two cases contained, and his suspicions had become a certainty when he saw Sir John Malyoe struck all white at being threatened about them, his face lowering so malevolently as to look murderous had he dared do it. But what were suspicions, or even certainty, compared to what Barnaby True's two eyes beheld when that man lifted the lids of the two cases—the locks having already been forced—and, flinging back first one lid and then the other, displayed to Barnaby's astonished sight a great treasure of gold and silver! Most of it was tied up in leather bags, but many of the coins, big and little, yellow and white, were lying loose and scattered about like so many beans, brimming the cases to the very top.

Barnaby sat dumbstruck at what he beheld. He sat staring at that marvelous treasure like a man in a trance, until, after a few seconds of this golden display, the pirate banged down the lids again and burst out laughing, and then Barnaby came back to himself with a jump.

"Well, and what do you think of that?" said the pirate. "Is it not enough for a man to turn pirate for? But," he continued, "it is not for the sake of showing you this that I have been waiting for you here so long, but to tell you that you are not the only passenger aboard, but that there is another, whom I am to confide to your care and attention, according to orders I have received. So, if you are ready, Master Barnaby, I'll fetch her in now." He waited for a moment, as though for Barnaby to speak; but Barnaby not replying, he arose and, putting away the bottle of grog and the glasses, crossed the saloon to a door like that from which Barnaby had come a little while before. This he opened, and after a moment's delay and a few words spoken to someone within, ushered from there a young lady, who came out very slowly into the saloon where Barnaby still sat at the table.

It was Marjorie Malyoe, very white, and looking as though stunned or bewildered by all that had befallen her.

Barnaby True could never tell whether the amazing, strange voyage that followed was of long or of short duration, whether it occupied three days or ten days. For conceive of two people of flesh and blood moving and living continually in all the circumstances and surroundings as of a nightmare dream, yet the two of them so happy together that all the universe was of no concern to them! How was anyone to tell whether in such circumstances any time appeared to be long or short? Does a dream appear to be long or to be short?

The vessel in which they sailed was a brigantine of good size and build, but manned by a considerable crew, the most strange and outlandish in their appearance that Barnaby had ever beheld— some white, some yellow, some black, and all tricked out with bright colors, and gold earrings in their ears, and some with great long mustaches, and others with handkerchiefs tied around their heads, and all talking a language together of which Barnaby True could understand not a single word, but which might have been Portuguese from one or two phrases he caught. Nor did this strange, mysterious crew, of who knows what sort of men, seem to pay any attention whatever to Barnaby or to the young lady. They might now and then have looked at him and her out of the corners of their yellow eyes, but that was all; otherwise they were indeed like the creatures of a dream. Only he who was the captain of this outlandish crew would maybe speak to Barnaby a few words as to the weather or what-not when he would come down into the saloon to mix a glass of grog or to light a pipe of tobacco, and then to go on deck again about his business. Otherwise Barnaby and the young lady were left to themselves, to do as they pleased, with no one to interfere with them.

As for her, she at no time showed any great sign of terror or of fear and only for a little while was numb and quiet, as though dazed with what had happened to her. Indeed, it is probable that wild beast, her grandfather, had so crushed her spirit by his tyranny and his violence that nothing that happened to her might seem sharp and keen, as it does to others of an ordinary sort.

But this was only at first, for afterward her face began to grow clear, as with a white light, and she would sit quite still, permitting Barnaby to gaze, for who knows how long, into her eyes, her face so transfigured and her lips smiling, and neither of them breathing, but hearing, as in another far-distant place, the outlandish jargon of the crew talking together in the warm, bright sunlight, or the sound of creaking block and tackle as they hauled upon the sheets.

Is it, then, any wonder that Barnaby True could never remember whether such a voyage as this was long or short?

It was as though they might have sailed so upon that wonderful voyage forever. You may guess how amazed was Barnaby True when, coming upon deck one morning, he found the brigantine riding upon an even keel, at anchor off Staten Island, near a small village on the shore, and the well-known roofs and chimneys of New York town in plain sight across the water.

'Twas the last place in the world he had expected to see.

And, indeed, it did seem strange to lie there alongside Staten Island all that day, with New York town so near at hand and yet so impossible to reach. For whether he desired to escape or not, Barnaby True could not but observe that both he and the young lady were so closely watched that they might as well have been prisoners, tied hand and foot and laid in the hold, so far as any hope of getting away was concerned.

All that day there was a great deal of mysterious coming and going aboard the brigantine, and in the afternoon a sailboat went up to the town, carrying the captain, and with a huge load covered

Marjorie Malyoe would sit quite still,
permitting Barnaby True to gaze into her eyes.

over with a canvas sheet in the stern. What was so taken up to the town Barnaby did not then guess, but the boat did not return again till about sundown.

For the sun was just dropping below the water when the captain came aboard once more and, finding Barnaby on deck, asked him to come down into the saloon, where they found the young lady sitting, the broad light of the evening shining in through the skylight, and making it all pretty bright within.

The captain commanded Barnaby to be seated, for he had something important to say to him. As soon as Barnaby had taken his place alongside the young lady, he began very seriously, with a preface somewhat thus: "Though you may think me the captain of this brigantine, young gentleman, I am not really so, but am under orders, and so have only carried out those orders of a superior in all these things that I have done." He went on to say that there was one thing yet remaining for him to do, and that was the greatest thing of all. He said that Barnaby and the young lady had not been fetched away from the *Belle Helen* as they were by any mere chance of accident, but that 'twas all a plan laid by a head wiser than his, and carried out by one whom he must obey in all things. He said that he hoped that both Barnaby and the young lady would perform willingly what they would be now called upon to do, but that whether or not they did so willingly, they must do it, for that those were the orders of one who was not to be disobeyed.

You may guess how Barnaby held his breath at all this; but whatever might have been his expectations, the very wildest of them all did not reach to that which was demanded of him. "My orders are these," said the other, continuing. "I am to take you and the young lady ashore, and to see that you are married before I leave you; and to that end a very good, decent, honest minister who lives ashore in the village was chosen and hath been spoken to and is now, no doubt, waiting for you to come. Such are my orders, and this is the last thing I have been ordered to do. So now I will leave you alone together for five minutes to talk it over, but be quick about it, for whether you both are willing or not, this thing must be done."

Then he went away, as he had promised, leaving those two alone together, Barnaby like one turned into stone, and the young lady, her face turned away, flaming as red as fire in the fading light.

No one knows exactly what Barnaby said to her, nor what words he used, but only that, with neither beginning nor end, he told her that God knew he loved her with all his heart and soul, and that there was nothing in all the world for him but her; but, nevertheless, if she would not have it as had been ordered, and if she were not willing to marry him as she was bidden to do, he would rather die than lend himself to forcing her to do such a thing against her will. Nevertheless, he told her she must speak up and tell him yes or no, and that God knew he would give all the world if she would say yes.

All this and more he said in such a tumult of words that there was no order in their speaking, she sitting there, her bosom rising and falling as though her breath stifled her. Nor is it known exactly what she replied to him, but only this—that she said she would marry him. At this he took her into his arms and set his lips to hers, his heart nearly melting away in his bosom.

Soon the captain came back into the saloon again, to find Barnaby sitting there holding her hand—she with her face turned away, and his heart beating like a trip hammer—and so saw that all was settled as he would have it. He then wished them both joy, and gave Barnaby his hand.

The yawlboat belonging to the brigantine was ready and waiting alongside when they came upon deck, and immediately they descended to it and took their seats. So they landed, and in a little

while were walking up the village street in the darkness, she clinging to his arm as though she would swoon, and the captain of the
brigantine and two other men from aboard following after them.
They soon arrived at the minister's house, finding him waiting for
them, smoking his pipe in the warm evening and walking up and
down in front of his own door. He immediately conducted them
into the house, where, his wife having fetched a candle, and two
others of the village folk being present, the good man having asked
several questions as to their names and their age and where they
were from, the ceremony was performed, and the certificate signed
by those present—except for the men who had come ashore from
the brigantine, and who refused to set their hands to any paper.

The same sailboat that had taken the captain up to the town in
the afternoon was waiting for them at the landing place. The captain having wished them Godspeed, and having shaken Barnaby
very heartily by the hand, they pushed off and, coming about, ran
away with the slant of the wind, dropping the shore and those
strange beings alike behind them into the night.

As they sped away through the darkness they could hear the
creaking of the sails being hoisted aboard the brigantine and so
knew that she was about to put to sea once more. Nor did Barnaby
True ever set eyes upon those beings again, nor is it likely that
anyone else ever did.

It was near midnight when they arrived at Mr. Hartright's wharf
at the foot of Wall Street, and so the streets were all dark and silent
and deserted as they walked up to Barnaby's home.

One can imagine the wonder and amazement of Barnaby's stepfather when, clad in a dressing gown and carrying a lighted candle
in his hand, he unlocked and unbarred the door, and so saw who it
was who had aroused him at such an hour of the night, and the
young and beautiful lady whom Barnaby had brought with him.

The first thought of the good man was that the *Belle Helen* had come into port. Nor did Barnaby contradict this idea as he led the way into the house, but waited until they were all safe and sound in private together before he unfolded his strange and wonderful story.

"This was left for you by two foreign sailors this afternoon, Barnaby," the good old man said, as he led the way through the hall, holding up the candle at the same time, so that Barnaby might see an object that stood by the door of the dining room.

Nor could Barnaby refrain from crying out with amazement when he saw that it was one of the two chests of treasure that Sir John Malyoe had fetched from Jamaica, and which the pirates had taken from the *Belle Helen*. As for Mr. Hartright, he guessed no more what was in it than the man in the moon.

The next day brought the *Belle Helen* herself into port, with the terrible news not only of having been attacked at night by pirates, but also that Sir John Malyoe was dead. For whether it was the sudden shock of the sight of his old captain's face—whom he himself had murdered and thought dead and buried—flashing out against the darkness, or whether it was the strain of the passion that overwhelmed his mind, it is certain that when the pirates left the *Belle Helen*, carrying with them the young lady and Barnaby and the traveling trunks, those left aboard the *Belle Helen* found Sir John Malyoe lying in a fit upon the floor, frothing at the mouth and blue in the face, as though he had been choked, and so took him away to his berth, where, the next morning about ten o'clock, he died, without once having opened his eyes or spoken a single word.

As for the villain manservant, no one ever saw him afterward; though whether he jumped overboard, or whether the pirates who so attacked the ship had carried him away bodily, who shall say?

After he had heard Barnaby's story, Mr. Hartright had been very uncertain as to the rightful ownership of the chest of treasure that had been left by those men for Barnaby, but the news of the death of Sir John Malyoe made the matter very easy for him to decide. For surely if that treasure did not belong to Barnaby, there could be no doubt that it must belong to his wife, she being Sir John Malyoe's legal heir. And so it was that that great fortune came to Barnaby True, the grandson of that famous pirate, William Brand. The English estate in Devonshire descended to Captain Malyoe, whom the young lady was to have married.

As for the other case of treasure, it was never heard of again, nor could Barnaby ever guess whether it was divided as booty among the pirates, or whether they had carried it away with them to some strange and foreign land, there to share it among themselves.

And so comes the end of the story, with only this to observe: that whether that strange appearance of Captain Brand's face by the light of the pistol was a ghostly and spiritual appearance, or whether he was present in flesh and blood, there is only to say that he was never heard of again; nor had he ever been heard of till that time since the day he was so shot from behind by Captain John Malyoe on the banks of the Rio Cobra River in the year 1733.

Buccaneers and Marooners
of the Spanish Main

Just above the northwestern shore of the old island of Hispaniola
—the Santo Domingo of our day—and separated from it only
by a narrow channel of some five or six miles in width, lies a
small island, known as the Tortuga de Mar, or Sea Turtle, because
of a distant resemblance to that animal. It is not more than twenty
miles in length by perhaps seven or eight in width; it is only a little
spot of land, and as you look at it upon the map a pin's head would
almost cover it. Yet from that spot, as from a center of inflamma-
tion, a burning fire of human wickedness and ruthlessness overran
the world, and spread terror and death throughout the Spanish
West Indies, from St. Augustine to the island of Trinidad, and from
Panama to the coasts of Peru.

About the middle of the seventeenth century certain French adventurers set out from the fortified island of St. Christopher in
longboats, directing their course westward, there to discover new
islands. Sighting Hispaniola "with abundance of joy," they landed,
and went into the country, where they found great quantities of
wild cattle, horses, and pigs. Vessels on the return voyage to Europe
from the West Indies needed resupplying, and food, especially
meat, was at a premium in the islands of the Spanish Main; therefore a great profit was to be made in preserving beef and pork, and
selling the meat to homeward-bound vessels.

81

The northwestern shore of Hispaniola, lying as it does at the eastern outlet of the old Bahama Channel, running between the island of Cuba and the great Bahama Banks, lay almost in the very main stream of travel. The pioneer Frenchmen were not slow to discover the double advantage to be gained from the wild cattle that cost them nothing to procure. So down upon Hispaniola they came by boatloads and shiploads, gathering like a swarm of mosquitoes, and overrunning the whole western end of the island. There they established themselves, spending the time alternately in hunting the wild cattle and buccanning* the meat, and squandering their hardly earned gains in wild behavior, the opportunities for which were never lacking in the Spanish West Indies.

At first the Spaniards thought nothing of the few travel-worn Frenchmen who dragged their longboats up on the beach, and shot a wild steer or two to keep body and soul together; but when the few grew to dozens, and the dozens to scores, and the scores to hundreds, it was a very different matter, and wrathful grumblings and mutterings began to be heard among the original settlers.

But of this the careless buccaneers never gave a thought. The only thing that troubled them was the lack of a more convenient shipping point than the main island offered.

This lack was at last filled by a party of hunters who ventured across the narrow channel that separated the main island from Tortuga. Here they found exactly what they needed—a good harbor, just at the junction of the Windward Channel with the old Bahama Channel—a spot where four-fifths of the Spanish-Indian trade would pass by their very wharves.

There were a few Spaniards upon the island, but they were a quiet folk, and well disposed to make friends with the strangers. But when more Frenchmen and still more Frenchmen crossed the

---

* Buccanning, by which the buccaneers gained their name, was a process of curing thin strips of meat by salting, smoking, and drying in the sun.

narrow channel, until they overran the Tortuga and turned it into one great curing house for the beef which they shot upon the neighboring island, the Spaniards grew restive over the matter, just as they had done upon the larger island.

One fine day there came half-a-dozen great boatloads of armed Spaniards, who landed upon the Turtle's Back and sent the Frenchmen flying to the woods and rocks. That night the Spaniards drank themselves mad and shouted themselves hoarse over their victory, while the beaten Frenchmen sullenly paddled their canoes back to the main island again, and the Sea Turtle was Spanish once more.

But the Spaniards were not contented with such a petty triumph as that of sweeping the island of Tortuga free from the obnoxious strangers. Down upon Hispaniola they came, flushed with their easy victory, and determined to root out every Frenchman, until not one single buccaneer remained. For a time they had an easy thing of it, for each French hunter roamed the woods by himself, with no better company than his half-wild dogs, so that when two or three Spaniards would meet such a one, he seldom if ever came out of the woods again, and even his resting place was lost.

But the very success of the Spaniards brought their ruin along with it, for the buccaneers began to combine together for self-protection, and out of that combination arose a strange union of lawless man with lawless man. When two entered upon this comradeship, articles were drawn up and signed by both parties, a common stock was made of all their possessions, and out into the woods they went to seek their fortunes; from then on, they were as one man: what one suffered, the other suffered; what one gained, the other gained. The only separation that came between them was death, and then the survivor inherited all that the other left.

As the French became more strongly organized for mutual self-protection, they assumed the offensive. Then down they came upon Tortuga, and now it was the turn of the Spanish to be hunted off the island like vermin, and the turn of the French to shout their victory.

Having firmly established themselves, a governor was sent to the French of Tortuga, one M. le Passeur, from the island of Saint Christopher. The Sea Turtle was fortified, and colonists, consisting of men and women of doubtful character, began pouring in upon the island, for it was said that the buccaneers thought no more of a doubloon-coin than of a Lima bean, so that this was the place for saloons to reap their golden harvest, and the island remained French.

Before this the Tortugans had been content to gain as much as possible from the homeward-bound vessels through the orderly channels of legitimate trade. It was reserved for Pierre le Grand to introduce piracy as a quicker and easier road to wealth than the semihonest exchange they had been used to practice.

Gathering together twenty-eight other spirits as hardy and reckless as himself, he put boldly out to sea in a boat hardly large enough to hold his crew. Running down the Windward Channel and out into the Caribbean Sea, he lay in wait for a prize that might be worth the risks of winning.

For a while their luck was steadily against them. Their provisions and water began to fail, and they saw nothing before them but starvation or a humiliating return. In this extremity they sighted a Spanish ship belonging to a fleet which had become separated from her consorts.

The boat in which the buccaneers sailed might, perhaps, have served for the great ship's longboat; the Spaniards out-numbered them three to one, and Pierre and his men were armed only with pistols and cutlasses. Nevertheless this was their one and only chance, and they determined to take the Spanish ship or to die in the attempt. Down upon the Spaniards they bore through the dusk of the night, and giving orders to the surgeon to sink their craft under them as they were leaving it, they swarmed up the side of the unsuspecting ship and upon its decks in a torrent—pistol in one hand and cutlass in the other. A part of them ran to the gunroom and secured the arms and ammunition, pistoling or cutting down all that stood in their way or offered opposition. The other party burst into the great cabin at the heels of Pierre le Grand, found the captain and a party of his friends at cards, set a pistol to his chest, and demanded that he surrender the ship. Nothing remained for the Spaniard but to yield, for there was no alternative between surrender and death. And so the great prize was won.

It was not long before the news of this exploit and of the vast treasure gained reached the ears of the buccaneers of Tortuga and Hispaniola. Then what a hubbub and an uproar and a tumult there was! Hunting wild cattle and buccanning the meat was at a discount, and the one and only thing to do was to go pirating; for where one such prize had been won, others were to be had.

In a short time freebooting assumed all of the routine of a regular business. Articles were drawn up between captain and crew, compacts were sealed, and agreements were entered into by the one party and the other.

In all professions there are those who make their mark, those who succeed only moderately well, and those who fail more or less entirely. Nor did pirating differ from this general rule, for in it were men who rose to distinction, men whose names, somewhat tarnished and rusted by the lapse of years, have come down even to us of the present day.

Pierre François, with his boatload of twenty-six desperadoes, ran boldly into the midst of the pearl fleet off the coast of South America, attacked the flagship under the very guns of two men-of-war, captured his ship—though she was armed with eight guns and manned with sixty men—and would have got her safely away, except that in having to put on sail, their mainmast went by the board, and then the men-of-war reached them, and their efforts were defeated.

But even though there were two men-of-war against all that remained of twenty-six buccaneers, the Spaniards were glad enough to make terms with them for the surrender of the vessel, and Pierre François and his men came off scot-free.

Bartholomew Portuguese was a worthy of even more note. In a boat manned with thirty fellow adventurers he fell upon a great ship off Cape Corrientes, manned with seventy men, all told.

He assaulted the ship again and again, and was beaten off with the pressure of numbers, only to renew the assault, until the Spaniards who survived, some fifty in all, surrendered to twenty living pirates, who poured upon their decks like a score of blood-stained, powder-grimed devils.

They lost their vessel by recapture, and Bartholomew Portuguese barely escaped with his life through a series of almost unbelievable adventures. But no sooner had he fairly escaped from the clutches of the Spaniards than, gathering together another band of adventurers, he fell upon the very same vessel in the gloom of the night, recaptured her when she rode at anchor in the harbor of Campeche under the guns of the fort, slipped the cable, and got away without the loss of a single man. He lost her in a hurricane soon afterward, just off the Isle of Pines; but the deed was no less daring for all that.

Another notable no less famous than these two pirates was Roch Braziliano, the savage Dutchman who came up from the coast of Brazil to the Spanish Main with a name ready-made for him. Upon the very first adventure which he undertook, he captured a money-ship of fabulous value and brought her safely into Jamaica. When at last captured by the Spaniards, he frightened them into letting him go by ferocious threats of vengeance from his followers.

Such were three of the pirate buccaneers who infested the Spanish Main. And there were hundreds of others no less desperate, no less reckless, no less relentless in their lust for plunder.

The effects of this freebooting soon became apparent. The risks to be assumed by the owners of vessels and the shippers of merchandise became so enormous that Spanish commerce was practically swept away from these waters. No vessel dared to venture out of port except under escort of powerful men-of-war, and even then they were not always secure from molestation. Exports from Central and South America were sent to Europe by way of the Strait of Magellan, and little or none went through the passes between the Bahamas and the Caribbees.

So at last buccaneering, as it had come to be generically called, ceased to pay the vast dividends that it had done at first. The cream was skimmed off, and only very thin milk was left in the dish. Fabulous fortunes were no longer earned in a ten days' cruise, and what money was won hardly paid for the risks of the winning. There had to be a new approach, or buccaneering would cease to exist.

Then arose one who showed the buccaneers a new way to squeeze money out of the Spaniards. This man was an Englishman —Lewis Scot.

The stoppage of commerce on the Spanish Main had naturally tended to accumulate all the wealth gathered and produced into the chief fortified cities and towns of the West Indies. As there no longer existed prizes upon the sea, they must be gained upon the land if they were to be gained at all. Lewis Scot was the first to appreciate this fact.

Gathering together a large and powerful body of men as hungry for plunder and as desperate as himself, he descended upon the town of Campeche, which he captured and sacked, stripping it of everything that could possibly be carried away.

When the town was cleared to the bare walls Scot threatened to set the torch to every house in the place if it was not ransomed by a large sum of money which he demanded. With this booty he set sail for Tortuga, where he arrived safely—and the problem was solved.

After him came one Mansvelt, a buccaneer of lesser note, who first made a descent upon the isle of Saint Catherine, now Old Providence, which he took; with this as a base, he made an unsuccessful descent upon Neuva Granada and Cartagena. His name might not have been handed down to us along with others of greater fame had he not been the master of that most apt of pupils, the great Captain Henry Morgan, most famous of all the buccaneers, one-time governor of Jamaica, and knighted by King Charles II.

After Mansvelt, there followed the bold John Davis, a native of Jamaica. With only eighty men, he swooped down upon the great city of Nicaragua in the darkness of the night, silenced the sentry with the thrust of a knife, and then began pillaging the churches and houses "without any respect or veneration."

Within a short time the whole town was in an uproar of alarm, and there was nothing left for the handful of men to do but to make their way to their boats. They were only in the town a short time, but in that time they were able to gather together and to carry away money and jewels to the value of fifty thousand pieces of eight, besides dragging off with them a dozen or more notable prisoners, whom they held for ransom.

And now one appeared upon the scene who reached a far greater height than any had arisen to before. This was François l'Olonoise, who sacked the great city of Maracaibo and the town of Gibraltar. Cold, unimpassioned, pitiless, his sluggish blood was never moved by one single pulse of human warmth, his icy heart was never touched by one ray of mercy or one spark of pity for the hapless wretches who chanced to fall into his bloody hands.

Against him the governor of Havana sent out a great war vessel, and with it an executioner, so that there might be no inconvenient delays of law after the pirates had been captured. But l'Olonoise did not wait for the coming of the war vessel; he went out to meet it, and he found it where it lay riding at anchor in the mouth of the river Estra. At the next dawn he made his attack—sharp, unexpected, decisive. In a little while the Spaniards were forced below the hatches, and the vessel was taken. Then came the end. One by one the poor shrieking wretches were dragged up from below, and one by one they were butchered in cold blood, while l'Olonoise stood upon the deck and looked coldly down upon what was being done. Among the rest the executioner was dragged upon the deck. He begged and implored that his life might be spared, promising to tell all that might be asked of him. L'Olonoise questioned him, and when he had squeezed him dry, waved his hand coldly, and the poor man went with the rest. Only one man was spared; him he sent to the governor of Havana with a message that from that time on he would show no mercy to any Spaniard whom he might meet in arms—a message which was not an empty threat.

The rise of l'Olonoise was by no means rapid. He worked his way up by hard labor and through much ill fortune. But, after many reverses, the tide turned and carried him with it from one success to another to the bitter end.

Cruising off Maracaibo, he captured a rich prize laden with a vast amount of ready money, and there conceived the idea of descending upon the powerful town of Maracaibo itself. Without loss of time he gathered together five hundred picked scoundrels from Tortuga, and taking with him one Michael de Basco as land captain, and two hundred more buccaneers whom he commanded, down he came into the Gulf of Venezuela and upon the doomed city like a blast of the plague. Leaving their vessels, the buccaneers made a land attack upon the fort that stood at the mouth of the inlet that led into Lake Maracaibo and guarded the city.

The Spaniards held out well, and fought with all the might that Spaniards possess; but after a fight of three hours all was given up and the garrison fled, spreading terror and confusion before them. As many of the inhabitants of the city as could do so escaped in boats to Gibraltar, which lies southward, on the shores of Lake Maracaibo, at a distance of some forty leagues or more.

Then the pirates marched into the town, and what followed may be conceived. It was a holocaust of passion and of blood such as even the Spanish West Indies had never seen before. Houses and churches were sacked until nothing was left but the bare walls; men and women were tortured to compel them to disclose where more treasure lay hidden.

Then, having wrenched all that they could from Maracaibo, they entered the lake and descended upon Gibraltar, where the rest of the panic-stricken inhabitants were huddled together in blind terror.

The governor of Merida, a brave soldier who had served his king in Flanders, had gathered together a troop of eight hundred men, had fortified the town, and now lay in wait for the coming of the pirates. The pirates soon arrived, and then, in spite of the brave defense, Gibraltar also fell. Then followed a repetition of the scenes that had been enacted in Maracaibo for the past fifteen days, only here they remained for four horrible weeks, extorting money— money, ever money!—from the poor poverty-stricken, pest-ridden souls crowded into that fever-hole of a town.

Then they left, but before they went they demanded still more money—ten thousand pieces of eight—as a ransom for the town, which otherwise should be given to the flames. There was some hesitation on the part of the Spaniards, some disposition to haggle, but there was no hesitation on the part of l'Olonoise. The torch *was* set to the town as he had promised, and at that the money was promptly paid, and the pirates were piteously begged to help quench the spreading flames. This they were pleased to do, but in spite of all their efforts nearly half of the town was consumed.

After that they returned to Maracaibo again, where they demanded a ransom of thirty thousand pieces of eight for the city. There was no haggling here, thanks to the fate of Gibraltar; only it was utterly impossible to raise that much money in all of the poverty-stricken region. But at last the matter was compromised, and the town was redeemed for twenty thousand pieces of eight and five hundred head of cattle, and tortured Maracaibo was free of them.

In the Ile de la Vache the buccaneers shared among themselves 260,000 pieces of eight, besides jewels and bales of silk and linen and miscellaneous plunder to a vast amount.

Such was the one great deed of l'Olonoise; from that time his star steadily declined—for even nature seemed to be fighting against such a monster—until at last he died a miserable, nameless death at the hands of an unknown tribe of Indians upon the Isthmus of Darien.

And now we come to the greatest of all the buccaneers, he who stands preeminent among them, and whose name even to this day is a charm to call up his deeds of daring, his dauntless courage, his ferocious cruelty, and his never-ending lust for gold—Captain Henry Morgan, the bold Welshman, who brought buccaneering to the height and flower of its glory.

Having sold himself, in the manner of the times, for his passage across the seas, he worked out his time of servitude at Barbados. As soon as he had regained his liberty he entered upon the trade of piracy, in which he soon reached a position of considerable prominence. He was associated with Mansvelt at the time of the latter's attack on Saint Catherine's Isle, the importance of which spot, as a center of operations against the neighboring coasts, Morgan never lost sight of.

The first attempt that Captain Henry Morgan ever made against any town in the Spanish Indies was the attack upon the city of Puerto del Principe in the island of Cuba, with a mere handful of men. It was a deed the boldness of which has never been outdone —not even by the famous attack upon Panama itself. Morgan and his men returned to their boats in the very face of the whole island of Cuba, aroused and determined upon their extermination. Not only did they make good their escape, but they brought away with them a vast amount of plunder, computed at three hundred thousand pieces of eight, besides five hundred head of cattle and many prisoners held for ransom.

But when the division of all this wealth came to be made, there were only fifty thousand pieces of eight to be found. What had become of the rest no man could tell but Captain Henry Morgan himself. Honesty among thieves was never a motto with him.

Rude, savage, and dishonest as Captain Morgan was, he seems to have had a wonderful power of persuading the wild buccaneers under him to submit everything to his judgment and to rely entirely on his word. In spite of the vast sum of money that he had evidently made away with, recruits poured in, until his band was larger and better equipped than ever.

And now it was determined that the plunder harvest was ripe at Portobelo, and that city's doom was sealed. The town was defended by two strong castles thoroughly manned, and officered by as gallant a soldier as ever carried Toledo steel at his side. But strong castles and gallant soldiers weighed not a barleycorn with the buccaneers when their blood was stirred by the lust of gold.

Landing at Puerto Naso, a town some ten leagues west of Portobelo, they marched to the latter town and, coming before the castle, boldly demanded its surrender. It was refused, and then

Morgan threatened that no mercy would be shown. Still surrender was refused; and then the castle was attacked and, after a bitter struggle, was captured. Morgan was as good as his word: every man in the castle was shut in the guard room, the match was set to the powder magazine, and soldiers, castle, and all were blown into the air, while through all the smoke and the dust the buccaneers poured into the town. Still the governor held out in the other castle; and he might have made good his defense, except that he was betrayed by the soldiers under him. Into the castle poured the howling buccaneers. But still the governor fought on, with his wife and daughter clinging to his knees and beseeching him to surrender, and the blood from his wounded forehead trickling down over his white collar, until a merciful bullet put an end to the vain struggle.

Here were enacted the old scenes—everything plundered that could be taken, and then a ransom set upon the town itself.

This time an honest, or an apparently honest, division was made of the spoils, which amounted to 250,000 pieces of eight, besides merchandise and jewels.

The next towns to suffer were poor Maracaibo and Gibraltar, now just beginning to recover from the desolation wrought by l'Olonoise. Once more both towns were plundered of every bit of merchandise and of every ounce of gold or silver, and once more both were ransomed until everything was squeezed from the wretched inhabitants.

Here the bold pirate's fortunes were likely to have changed, for when Captain Morgan came up from Gibraltar he found three great men-of-war lying in the entrance to the lake awaiting his coming. Seeing that he was hemmed in at the narrow sheet of water, Captain Morgan was inclined to compromise matters, even offering to relinquish all the plunder he had gained if he were allowed to depart in peace. But the Spanish admiral would hear nothing of this. Having the pirates, as he thought, securely in his grasp, he would relinquish nothing, but would sweep them from the face of the sea once and forever.

That was an unlucky determination for the Spaniards to reach, for instead of paralyzing the pirates with fear, as he expected it would do, it simply turned their mad courage into as mad desperation.

A great vessel that they had taken in the attack on the town of Maracaibo was converted into a fire ship, manned with logs of wood and filled with brimstone, pitch, and palm leaves soaked in oil. Then out of the lake the pirates sailed to meet the Spaniards, the fire ship leading the way and bearing down directly upon the admiral's vessel. At the helm stood volunteers, the most desperate and the bravest of all the pirate gang, and at the ports stood the logs of wood. So they came up with the admiral, and grappled with his ship in spite of the thunder of all his great guns, and then the Spaniard saw, all too late, what his opponent really was.

He tried to swing loose, but almost instantly clouds of smoke and a mass of roaring flames enveloped both vessels, and the admiral was lost. The second vessel, not wishing to wait for the coming of the pirates, bore down upon the fort, under the guns of which the cowardly crew sank her and made their way to the shore. The third vessel, not having an opportunity to escape, was taken by the pirates without the slightest resistance, and the passage from the lake was cleared. So the buccaneers sailed away, leaving Maracaibo and Gibraltar plundered a second time.

And now Captain Morgan determined to undertake another venture, the like of which had never been equaled in all of the annals of buccaneering. This was nothing less than the descent upon and the capture of Panama, which was, next to Cartagena, perhaps, the most powerful and the most strongly fortified city in the West Indies.

In preparation for this venture he obtained letters of marque*
from the governor of Jamaica, by virtue of which commission he
began immediately to gather around him all material necessary for
the undertaking.

When it became known abroad that the great Captain Morgan
was about to undertake an adventure that was to eclipse all that
had ever been done before, great numbers came flocking to his
standard, until he had gathered together an army of two thousand
or more desperadoes and pirates, although the venture itself was
kept a total secret from everyone. Port Couillon, in the island of
Hispaniola, over against the Ile de la Vache, was the place of assem-
bly, and there the motley band gathered from all quarters. Provisions had been plundered from the mainland wherever they could
be obtained, and by the twenty-fourth of October 1670, everything
was ready.

The island of Saint Catherine was at one time captured by Mansvelt, Morgan's master in his trade of piracy. It had been retaken by
the Spaniards and was now thoroughly fortified by them. Almost
the first attempt that Morgan had made as a master pirate was the
retaking of Saint Catherine's Isle. In that undertaking he had
failed; but now, as there was an absolute need of some such place
as a base of operations, he determined that the place *must* be
taken. And it was taken.

The Spaniards, during the time of their possession, had fortified
it most thoroughly and completely, and had the governor there
been as brave as he who met his death in the castle of Portobelo,
there might have been a different tale to tell. As it was, he surrendered it in a most cowardly fashion, merely stipulating that there
should be a fake attack by the buccaneers, whereby his credit might
be saved. And so Saint Catherine was won.

* Written authority granted to a private individual to fit out an armed ship to
plunder the enemy.

Captain Henry Morgan recruited hundreds of desperadoes
and pirates for his attacks.

The next step to be taken was the capture of the castle of Chagres, which guarded the mouth of the river of that name; the buccaneers would be compelled to transport their troops and provisions up this river for the attack upon the city of Panama. This adventure was undertaken by four hundred picked men under command of Captain Morgan himself.

The castle of Chagres, known as San Lorenzo by the Spaniards, stood upon the top of a huge rock at the mouth of the river, and was one of the strongest fortresses for its size in all of the West Indies. This stronghold Morgan had to have if he ever hoped to win Panama.

The attack of the castle and the defense of it were equally fierce, bloody, and desperate. Again and again the buccaneers assaulted, and again and again they were beaten back. So the morning came, and it seemed as though the pirates had been baffled this time. But just at this juncture the thatch of palm leaves on the roofs of some of the buildings inside the fortifications took fire, and a conflagration followed, which caused the explosion of one of the gunpowder storerooms. In the paralysis of terror that followed, the pirates forced their way into the fortifications, and the castle was won. Most of the Spaniards flung themselves from the castle walls into the river or upon the rocks beneath, preferring death to capture and possible torture; many who were left were put to the sword, and some few were spared and held as prisoners.

So fell the castle of Chagres, and nothing now lay between the buccaneers and the city of Panama but the forests.

And now the name of the town whose doom was sealed was no secret.

Up the river of Chagres went Captain Henry Morgan and twelve hundred men, packed closely in their canoes; they never stopped, except now and then to rest their stiffened legs, until they had come to a place known as Cruz de San Juan Gallego, where they were compelled to leave their boats on account of the shallowness of the water.

Leaving a guard of 160 men to protect their boats as a place of refuge in case they should be attacked before Panama, they turned and plunged into the wilderness before them.

There a more powerful foe awaited them than a host of Spaniards with match, powder, and lead—starvation. They met little or no opposition in their progress; but wherever they turned they found every fiber of meat, every grain of maize, every ounce of bread or meal swept away or destroyed before them. Even when the buccaneers had successfully overcome an ambush or an attack, and had sent the Spaniards flying, the fugitives took the time to strip their dead comrades of every grain of food in their leather sacks, leaving nothing but the empty bags. They afterward resorted to eating even those leather bags, just so there would be something to ferment in their stomachs.

Ten days they struggled, forcing their way onward, faint with hunger and haggard with weakness and fever. Then, from the high hill and over the tops of the forest trees, they saw the steeples of Panama, and nothing remained between them and their goal but the fighting of four Spaniards to each one of them—a simple thing which they had done over and over again.

Down they poured upon Panama, and out came the Spaniards to meet them; 400 horse- and 2,500 foot-soldiers, and 2,000 wild bulls which had been herded together to be driven over the buccaneers so that their ranks might be disordered and broken. The buccaneers were only 800 strong; the others had either fallen in battle or had dropped along the dreary pathway through the wilderness; but in the space of two hours the Spaniards were flying madly over the plain, minus 600 who lay dead or dying behind them.

As for the bulls, as many of them as were shot served as food there and then for the half-famished pirates, for the buccaneers were never more at home than in the slaughter of cattle.

Then they marched toward the city. Three hours' more fighting and they were in the streets, howling, yelling, plundering, gorging, and giving full vent to all the vile emotions that burned in their hearts like a hell of fire. And now followed the usual sequence of events of cruelty and extortion; only this time there was no town to ransom, for Morgan had given orders that the city should be destroyed. The torch was set to it, and Panama, one of the greatest cities in the New World, was swept from the face of the earth. Why the deed was done no man but Morgan could tell; perhaps it was that all the secret hiding places for treasure might be brought to light. But whatever the reason was, it lay hidden in the breast of the great buccaneer himself. For three weeks Morgan and his men stayed in this dreadful place; and they marched away with 175 beasts of burden loaded with treasures of gold and silver and jewels, besides great quantities of merchandise, and six hundred prisoners held for ransom.

Whatever became of all that vast wealth, and what it amounted to, no man but Morgan ever knew, for when a division was made it was found that there was only *two hundred pieces of eight to each man.*

When this dividend was declared a howl of anger went up, under which even Captain Henry Morgan shuddered. At night he and four other commanders slipped their cables and ran out to sea, and it was said that these five men divided the greater part of the booty among themselves. But the wealth plundered at Panama could hardly have fallen short of a million and a half dollars. Computing it at this reasonable figure, the various prizes won by Henry Morgan in the West Indies would stand as follows: Panama, $1,500,000; Portobelo, $800,000; Puerto del Principe, $700,000; Maracaibo and Gibraltar, $400,000; various piracies, $250,000—making a grand

Captain Morgan and his men sacked Panama,
and marched away with treasures of gold, silver, and jewels,
and great quantities of merchandise.

total of $3,650,000 as the vast harvest of plunder. With this fabulous wealth, wrenched from the Spaniards by means of the rack and the cord, and pilfered from his companions by the meanest of thieving, Captain Henry Morgan retired from business, honored by all, rendered famous by his deeds, knighted by the good King Charles II, and finally appointed governor of the rich island of Jamaica.

Other buccaneers followed Captain Henry Morgan. Campeche was taken and sacked, and even Cartagena itself fell; but with Henry Morgan culminated the glory of the buccaneers, and from that time they declined in power and wealth and wickedness until they were finally swept away.

The governments in Europe, stirred at last by these outrageous barbarities, seriously undertook the suppression of the freebooters, cutting at the main trunk until its members were scattered, and it was thought that the organization was exterminated. But, far from being exterminated, the individual members were merely scattered north, south, east, and west, each forming a nucleus around which gathered and clustered the very worst of the debris of humanity.

The result was that when the seventeenth century was fairly packed away with its lavender in the store-chest of the past, twenty or more bands of freebooters were cruising along the Atlantic seaboard in armed vessels, each with a black flag with its skull and crossbones, and with a nondescript crew made up of the remnants of civilized and semicivilized humanity, known generally as marooners, swarming upon the decks below.

Nor did these offshoots from the old buccaneer stem confine their deeds to the American seas alone. The East Indies and the African coast also witnessed their doings, and suffered from them, and even the Bay of Biscay had good cause to remember more than one visit from them.

So up and down the Atlantic seaboard they cruised, and for the fifty years that marooning was in the flower of its glory it was a sorrowful time for the coasts of New England, the middle provinces, and the Virginias, sailing to the West Indies with their cargoes of salt fish, grain, and tobacco. Trading became almost as dangerous as privateering, and sea captains were chosen as much for their knowledge of the flintlock and the cutlass as for their seamanship.

As by far the largest part of the trading in American waters was conducted by these Yankee coasters, so by far the heaviest blows, and those most keenly felt, fell upon them. Bulletin after bulletin came into port with its sad tale of this vessel burned or that vessel sunk, this one held by the pirates for their own use or that one stripped of its goods and sent into port as empty as an eggshell from which the yolk had been sucked. Boston, New York, Philadelphia, and Charleston suffered alike, and worthy ship owners had to stop counting their losses on their fingers and take to the slate to keep the dismal record.

"*Maroon*—to put ashore on a desert isle, as a sailor, under pretense of having committed some great crime." Thus the good Noah Webster gives the dry bones, the anatomy, upon which the imagination may construct a specimen to suit itself.

It is from this word that the marooners took their name, for marooning was one of their most effective instruments of punishment or revenge. If a pirate broke one of the many rules which governed the particular band to which he belonged, he was marooned; did a captain defend his ship to such a degree as to be unpleasant to the pirates attacking it, he was marooned; even the pirate captain himself, if he displeased his followers by the severity of his rule, was in danger of having the same punishment visited upon him which he had perhaps more than once visited upon another.

The process of marooning was as simple as terrible. A suitable place was chosen—generally some desert isle as far removed as

Marooning a man on a barren isle was one of the pirates'
most effective instruments of punishment or revenge.

possible from the pathway of commerce—and the condemned man was rowed from the ship to the beach. Out he was bundled upon the sand spit; a gun, a half-dozen bullets, a few pinches of powder, and a bottle of water were hurled ashore after him, and away rowed the boat's crew back to the ship, leaving the poor wretch alone to rave away his life in madness, or to sit sunken in his gloomy despair till death mercifully released him from torment. It rarely if ever happened that anything was known of him after having been marooned. A boat's crew from some vessel, sailing by chance that way, might perhaps find a few chalky bones bleaching upon the white sand in the garish glare of the sunlight, but that was all. And such were marooners.

By far the largest number of pirate captains were Englishmen, for, from the days of good Queen Bess, English sea captains seemed to have a natural turn for any species of venture that had a smack of piracy in it, and from the great Admiral Drake of the old, old days, to the fierce Morgan of buccaneering times, the Englishman did the boldest and wickedest deeds, and wrought the most damage.

First of all upon the list of pirates stands the bold Captain Avary, one of the institutors of marooning. Him we see but dimly, half hidden by the glamouring mists of legends and tradition. Others who came afterward outstripped him far enough in their doings, but he stands preeminent as the first of marooners about whom history has passed down information.

When the English, Dutch, and Spanish entered into an alliance to suppress buccaneering in the West Indies, certain worthies of Bristol, in old England, fitted out two vessels to assist in this praiseworthy project; for certainly Bristol trade suffered from the Morgans and the l'Olonoises of that old time. One of these vessels was named the *Duke*, of which a certain Captain Gibson was the commander and Avary the mate.

Away they sailed to the West Indies, and there Avary became impressed by the advantages offered by piracy, and by the amount of good things that were to be gained by very little effort.

One night the captain (who was one of those fellows mightily addicted to punch), instead of going ashore to saturate himself with rum at the tavern, had his drink in his cabin in private. While he lay snoring away the effects of his rum in the cabin, Avary and a few other conspirators heaved the anchor very leisurely and sailed out of the harbor of Corunna and through the midst of the allied fleet riding at anchor in the darkness.

When the morning came, the captain was awakened by the pitching and tossing of the vessel, the rattle and clatter of the tackle overhead, and the noise of footsteps passing and repassing across the deck. Perhaps he lay for a while turning the matter over and over in his muddled head, but he soon rang the bell, and Avary and another fellow answered the call.

"What's the matter?" bawled the captain from his berth.

"Nothing," said Avary, coolly.

"Something's the matter with the ship," said the captain. "Does she drive? What weather is it?"

"Oh no," said Avary, "we are at sea."

"At sea?"

"Come, come!" said Avary. "I'll tell you; you must know that I'm the captain of the ship now, and you must be packing from this cabin. We are bound to Madagascar, to make all of our fortunes, and if you're a mind to ship for the cruise, why, we'll be glad to have you, if you will be sober and mind your own business; if not, there is a boat alongside, and I'll have you set ashore."

The poor half-tipsy captain had no relish to go pirating under the command of his backsliding mate, so out of the ship he bundled, and away he rowed with four or five of the crew, who, like him, refused to join with their jolly shipmates.

The rest of them sailed away to the East Indies, to try their fortunes in those waters, for Captain Avary was of high spirits, and had no mind to fritter away his time in the West Indies, squeezed dry by buccaneer Morgan and others. No, he would make a bold stroke for it at once.

On his way he recruited a couple of ships and crews similar to his own—two sloops off Madagascar. With these he sailed away to the coast of India, and for a time his name was lost in the obscurity of uncertain history. But only for a time, for suddenly it flamed out in a blaze of glory. It was reported that a vessel belonging to the great mogul, laden with treasure and bearing the monarch's own daughter upon a holy pilgrimage to Mecca (they being Mohammedans), had fallen in with the pirates, and after a short resistance had been surrendered, with the damsel, her court, and all the diamonds, pearls, silk, silver, and gold aboard. It was rumored that the great mogul, raging at the insult offered to him through his own flesh and blood, had threatened to wipe out of existence the few English settlements scattered along the coast. Rumor had it that Avary was going to marry the Indian princess and would turn rajah, and give up piracy as indecent. As for the treasure itself, there was no end to the extent to which it grew as it passed from mouth to mouth.

Cracking the nut of romance and exaggeration, we come to the kernel of the story—that Avary did fall in with an Indian vessel laden with great treasure (and possibly with the mogul's daughter), which he captured, and thereby gained a vast prize.

Having concluded that he had earned enough money by the trade he had undertaken, he determined to retire and live decently for the rest of his life upon what he already had. As a step toward this objective, he set about cheating his Madagascar partners out of their share of what had been gained. He persuaded them to store all the treasure in his vessel, it being the largest of the three. And

so, having it safely in hand, he altered the course of his ship one
fine night, and when the morning came the Madagascar sloops
found themselves floating upon a wide ocean without even one
coin of the treasure for which they had fought so hard, and for
which they might whistle for all the good it would do them.

At first Avary had a mind to settle at Boston, in Massachusetts,
and had that little town been one bit less bleak and forbidding, it
might have had the honor of being the home of this famous man.
As it was, he did not like the looks of it, so he sailed away eastward,
to Ireland, where he settled himself at Biddeford, in hopes of an
easy life of it for the rest of his days.

Here he found himself the possessor of a plentiful stock of jewels, such as pearls, diamonds, rubies, etc., but with hardly a handful
of honest coins to jingle in his breeches pocket. He consulted with
a certain merchant of Bristol concerning the disposal of the stones
—a fellow not much firmer in his habits of honesty than Avary
himself. This man undertook to act as Avary's broker. Off he
marched with the jewels, and that was the last that the pirate saw
of his Indian treasure.

Perhaps the most famous of all the piratical names to American
ears are those of Captain Robert Kidd and Captain Edward Teach,
or "Blackbeard."

Nothing will be ventured in regard to Kidd at this time, nor in
regard to the pros and cons as to whether he really was or was not a
pirate, after all. For many years he was the very hero of heroes of
piratical fame; there was hardly a creek or stream or point of land
along our coast, hardly a convenient bit of good sandy beach, or
hump of rock, or water-washed cave, where fabulous treasures were
not said to have been hidden by this worthy marooner. Now we are
assured that he never was a pirate, and never did bury any treasure,
except for a certain chest, which he was compelled to hide upon
Gardiner's Island—and perhaps even *it* was mythical.

For many years Captain Kidd was the very hero of heroes
of piratical fame, and it is said
he buried a certain chest on Gardiner's Island.

So poor Kidd must be relegated to the dull ranks of simply respectable people, or semirespectable people at best.

But with Blackbeard it is different, for in him we have a real, ranting, raging, roaring pirate—one who really did bury treasure, who made more than one captain walk the plank, and who committed more private murders than he could number on the fingers of both hands—one who fills, and will continue to fill, the place to which he has been assigned for generations.

Captain Teach was born in Bristol, and learned his trade on board various privateers in the East Indies during the old French war—that of 1702—and a better apprenticeship no man could serve. At last, somewhere around the latter part of the year 1716, a privateering captain, one Benjamin Hornigold, raised him from the ranks and put him in command of a sloop—a lately captured prize —and Blackbeard's fortune was made. It was a very slight step, and but the change of a few letters, to convert "privateer" into "pirate," and it was a very short time before Teach made that change. Not only did he make it himself, but he persuaded his old captain to join him.

And now began that series of bold and lawless deeds which have made his name so famous, and which place him among the very greatest of marooning freebooters.

"Our hero," says the old historian who sings of the arms and bravery of this great man—"our hero assumed the name of Blackbeard from that large quantity of hair which, like a frightful meteor, covered his whole face, and frightened America more than any comet that appeared there in a long time. He was accustomed to twist it with ribbons into small tails and turn them about his ears. In time of action he wore a sling over his shoulders, with three brace of pistols hanging in holsters; he stuck lighted matches under his hat, which, appearing on each side of his face, and his eyes naturally looking fierce and wild, made him altogether such a figure that imagination cannot form an idea of a Fury from hell to look more frightful."

The night before the day of the action in which he was killed he sat up drinking with some congenial company until broad daylight. One of them asked him if his poor young wife knew where his treasure was hidden. "No," said Blackbeard, "nobody but the Devil and I knows where it is, and the longest liver shall have all."

For a time Blackbeard worked at his trade down on the Spanish Main, gathering, in the few years he was there, a very neat little fortune in the booty captured from numerous vessels; but soon he took it into his head to try his luck along the coast of the Carolinas. So off he sailed to the north, with quite a respectable little fleet, consisting of his own vessel and two captured sloops. From that time he was actively engaged in making American history in his small way.

He first appeared off the bar of Charleston Harbor, to the excitement of the town, and there he lay for five or six days, blockading the port, and stopping incoming and outgoing vessels at his pleasure, so that, for the time, the commerce of the province was entirely paralyzed. All the vessels so stopped he held as prizes, and all the crews and passengers (among the latter of whom was more than one provincial notable of the day) he retained as though they were prisoners of war.

And it was a very awkward thing for the good folk of Charleston to behold, day after day, a black flag with its white skull and crossbones fluttering at the front of the pirate captain's craft, over across the level stretch of green salt marshes; and it was very unpleasant, too, to know that this or that prominent citizen was crowded down with the other prisoners under the hatches.

One morning Captain Blackbeard found that his stock of "medicine" was low. "Tut," said he, "we'll turn no hair gray for that!" So up he called the bold Captain Richards, the commander of his consort the *Revenge* sloop, and bid him take Mr. Marks (one of his prisoners) and go up to Charleston and get the medicine. There was no task that suited Captain Richards better than that. Up to the town he rowed, as bold as brass. "Look ye," said he to the governor, rolling his lump of tobacco from one cheek to another—"look ye, we're after this and that, and if we don't get it, why, I'll tell you plain, we'll burn them bloody crafts of yours that we've took over yonder, and cut the throat of every blockhead aboard 'em."

There was no answering an argument of such force as this, and the worshipful governor and the good folk of Charleston knew very well that Blackbeard and his crew were the men to do as they promised. So Blackbeard got his medicine, and though it cost the colony two thousand dollars—it was worth that much to the town to be quit of him.

They say that while Captain Richards was conducting his negotiations with the governor his boat's crew were stumping around the streets of the town, having a glorious time of it, while the good folk glowered wrathfully at them but dared say or do nothing.

Having gained a booty of between seven and eight thousand dollars from the prizes captured, the pirates sailed away from Charleston Harbor to the coast of North Carolina.

And now Blackbeard, following the plan adopted by so many others of his kind, began to work his brains for means to cheat his fellows out of their share of the booty.

At Topsail Inlet he ran his own vessel aground, as though by accident. Hands, the captain of one of the consorts, pretending to come to his assistance, also grounded *his* sloop. Nothing now remained but for those who were able to get away in the other craft, which was all that was now left of the little fleet. This Blackbeard did with some forty of his favorites. The rest of the pirates were left on the sand spit to await the return of their companions—which never happened.

As for Blackbeard and those who were with him, they were that much richer, for there were fewer pockets to fill. But there were still too many to share the booty, in Blackbeard's opinion, and so he marooned more of them—some eighteen or twenty—upon a naked sandbank, from which they were afterward mercifully rescued by another freebooter who chanced that way—a certain Major Stede Bonnet, of whom more will presently be said. About that time a royal proclamation had been issued offering pardon to all pirates in arms who would surrender to the king's authority before a given date. So up went Blackbeard to the governor of North Carolina and made his neck safe by surrendering to the proclamation—although he kept a tight hold upon what he had already gained.

Soon afterward Captain Blackbeard was established in the good province of North Carolina, where he and the governor struck up a vast deal of intimacy, as profitable as it was pleasant. There is something very pretty in the thought of the bold sea-rover giving up his adventurous life (except for now and then an excursion against a trader or two in the neighboring sound, when the need of money was pressing), settling quietly down into the routine of old colonial life, with a young wife of sixteen at his side, who made the fourteenth that he had in various ports here and there in the world.

Becoming tired of an inactive life, Blackbeard soon resumed his piratical career. He cruised around in the rivers and inlets and sounds of North Carolina for a while, ruling the roost and with never anyone to stop him, until there was no bearing such a pest any longer. So they sent a committee up to the governor of Virginia asking if he would help them in their trouble.

There were two men-of-war lying at Kicquetan, in the James River, at the time. To them the governor of Virginia applied, and plucky Lieutenant Maynard, of the *Pearl*, was sent to Ocracoke Inlet to fight this pirate who ruled down there like some emperor. There he found Blackbeard waiting for him, and as ready for a fight as ever the lieutenant himself could be. Fight they did, and while it lasted it was as pretty a piece of business of its kind as one could wish to see. Blackbeard drained a glass of grog, wishing the lieutenant luck in getting alongside him, fired a broadside, blew some twenty of the lieutenant's men out of existence, and totally crippled one of his little sloops for the balance of the fight. After that, and under cover of the smoke, the pirate and his men boarded the other sloop, and then followed a fine old-fashioned hand-to-hand conflict between him and the lieutenant. First they fired their pistols, and then they went at it with cutlasses—right, left, up and down, cut and slash—until the lieutenant's cutlass broke off at the hilt. Blackbeard would have finished him off handsomely, but up stepped one of the lieutenant's men and gave him a great slash across the neck, so that the lieutenant came off with no more injury than a cut over the knuckles.

At the first discharge of their pistols Blackbeard had been shot through the body, but he was not giving up for that—not he. He was of the true roaring, raging breed of pirates, and stood up to it until he received twenty more cutlass cuts and five additional shots, and then fell dead while trying to fire off an empty pistol. After that the lieutenant cut off the pirate's head, and sailed away in triumph, with the bloody trophy nailed to the bow of his battered sloop.

Those of Blackbeard's men who were not killed were carried off to Virginia, and all of them tried and hanged but one or two, their names, no doubt, still standing in a row in the provincial records.

But did Blackbeard really bury treasures, as tradition says, along the sandy shores he haunted?

Master Clement Downing, midshipman aboard the *Salisbury*, wrote a book after his return from the cruise to Madagascar, to where the *Salisbury* had been ordered, to put an end to the piracy with which those waters were infested. He says:

"At Guzarat I met with a Portuguese named Anthony de Sylvestre; he came with two other Portuguese and two Dutchmen to take on in the Moor's service, as many Europeans do. This Anthony told me he had been among the pirates, and that he belonged to one of the sloops in Virginia when Blackbeard was taken. He informed me that if it should be my lot ever to go to York River or Maryland, near an island called Mulberry Island, provided we went on shore at the watering place, where the shipping used most commonly to ride, that there the pirates had buried considerable sums of money in great chests well clamped with iron plates. As to my part, I never was that way, nor much acquainted with any that ever used those parts; but I have made inquiry, and am informed that there is such a place as Mulberry Island. If any person who uses those parts should think it worthwhile to dig a little way at the upper end of a small cove, where it is convenient to land, he would soon find whether the information I had was well grounded. Fronting the landing place are five trees, among which, he said, the money was hid. I cannot warrant the truth of this account; but if I was ever to go there, I should find some means or other to satisfy myself, as it could not be a great deal out of my way. If anybody should obtain the benefit of this account, if it please God that they ever come to England, 'tis hoped they will remember whence they had this information."

Another worthy was Captain Edward Low, who learned his trade of sail-making at good old Boston town, and piracy at Honduras. No one stood higher in the trade than he, and no one mounted to more lofty altitudes of bloodthirsty and unscrupulous wickedness. 'Tis strange that so little has been written and sung of this man of might, for he was as worthy of story and of song as was Blackbeard.

It was under a Yankee captain that he made his first cruise— down to Honduras, for a cargo of logwood, which in those times was no better than stolen from the Spanish folk.

Buccaneers and Marooners of the Spanish Main

Buccaneers and Marooners of the Spanish Main

One day, lying off the shore, in the Gulf of Honduras, came Edward Low and the crew of the whaleboat rowing across from the beach, where they had been all morning chopping logwood.

"What are you after?" said the captain, for they were coming back with nothing but themselves in the boat.

"We're after our dinner," said Low, as spokesman of the party.

"You'll have no dinner," said the captain, "until you fetch another load."

"Dinner or no dinner, we'll pay for it," said Low, who raised his musket, squinted along the barrel, and pulled the trigger.

Luckily the gun misfired, and the Yankee captain was spared to steal logwood a while longer.

All the same, that was no place for Ned Low to make a longer stay, so off he and his messmates rowed in a whaleboat, captured a brig out at sea, and turned pirates.

He soon fell in with the notorious Captain Lowther, a fellow of his own kind, who put the finishing touches to his education and taught him what wickedness he did not already know.

And so he became a master pirate, and a famous hand at his craft, and thereafter forever bore hatred for all Yankees because of the dinner he had lost, and never failed to smite whatever one of them luck put within his reach. Once he fell in with a ship off South Carolina—the *Amsterdam Merchant*, Captain Williamson, commander—a Yankee craft and a Yankee master. He slit the nose and cropped the ears of the captain, and then sailed merrily away, feeling the better for having marred a Yankee.

New York and New England had more than one visit from the valiant captain, each of which visits they had good cause to remember, for he made them suffer.

In the year 1722 thirteen vessels were riding at anchor in front of the good town of Marblehead. Into the harbor sailed a strange craft. "Who is she?" said the townsfolk, for the coming of a new vessel was no small matter in those days.

Who the strangers were was not long a matter of doubt. Up went the black flag, with the skull and crossbones facing front.

" 'Tis the bloody Low," said one and all. Immediately all was flutter and commotion, as in a duck pond when a hawk dives and strikes in the midst.

It was a glorious thing for the captain, for here were thirteen Yankee crafts at one and the same time. So he took what he wanted, and then sailed away, and it was many a day before Marblehead forgot that visit.

Some time after this he and his companion ship fell foul of an English sloop of war, the *Greyhound*, by which they were so roughly handled that Low was glad enough to slip away, leaving his consort ship and her crew behind him, as a sop to the powers of law and order. And lucky for them if no worse fate awaited them than to walk the dreadful plank with a bandage around the blinded eyes and a rope around the elbows. So the consort was taken, and the crew tried and hanged in chains, and Low sailed off in as pretty a bit of rage as ever a pirate fell into.

The end of this pirate is lost in the fogs of the past. Some say that he died of yellow fever down in New Orleans; that it was not at the end of a hangman's noose, more's the pity.

Here fittingly with strictly American pirates should stand Major Stede Bonnet along with the rest. But in truth he was only a poor half-and-half fellow of his kind, and even after his hand was turned to the business he had undertaken, a qualm of conscience would now and then come across him, and he would make vast promises to forswear his evil courses.

However, he jogged along in his course of piracy snugly enough until he fell foul of the gallant Colonel Rhett, off Charleston Harbor, when his luck and his courage both were suddenly snuffed out with a puff of powder smoke and a good rattling broadside. Down

Lucky for the prisoners if no worse fate awaited them
than to walk the dreadful plank with a bandage around the eyes
and a rope around the elbows.

came the Black Roger with its skull and crossbones from the fore, and Colonel Rhett had the glory of fetching back as pretty a cargo of scoundrels and cutthroats as the town ever saw.

After the next court sessions they were tried and strung up, all in a row—evil apples ready for the roasting.

Ned England was a fellow of different blood—only he snapped his whip across the back of society over in the East Indies and along the hot shores of Hindustan.

The name of Captain Howel Davis stands high among his fellows. He was the Ulysses of pirates, the beloved not only of Mercury, but of Minerva.

He it was who hoodwinked the captain of a French ship of double the size and strength of his own, and fairly cheated him into the surrender of his craft without the firing of a single pistol or the striking of a single blow. He it was who sailed boldly into the port of Gambia, on the coast of Guinea, and under the guns of the castle proclaimed himself as a merchant trading for slaves.

The deception was kept up until the fruit of mischief was ripe for the picking. Then, when the governor and the guards of the castle were lulled into security, and when Davis's band was scattered about wherever each man could do the most good, it was out pistol, up cutlass, and death if a finger moved. They tied the soldiers back to back, and the governor to his own armchair, and then rifled wherever it pleased them. After that they sailed away, and though they had not made the fortune they had hoped to attain, it was a good snug, round sum that they shared among them.

Their courage growing high with success, they determined to raid the island of Principe—a prosperous Portuguese settlement on the coast. The plan for taking the place was cleverly laid, and would have succeeded, only that a Portuguese among the pirate crew turned traitor and carried the news ashore to the governor of the fort. The next day, when Captain Davis came ashore, he found stationed there a good strong guard, as though to honor his coming. But after he and those with him were out of their boat, and well away from the water side, there was a sudden rattle of musketry, a cloud of smoke, and a dull groan or two. Only one man ran out from under that pungent cloud, jumped into the boat, and rowed away; and when it lifted, there lay Captain Davis and his companions all in a heap, like a pile of old clothes.

Captain Bartholomew Roberts was the particular and special pupil of Davis, and when that worthy met his death so suddenly and so unexpectedly in the unfortunate manner just described, he was chosen unanimously as the captain of the fleet; he was a worthy pupil of a worthy master. Many were the poor fluttering merchant ducks that this sea hawk swooped upon and struck; and cleanly and cleverly were they plucked before his savage grip loosened its hold upon them.

"He made a gallant figure," says the old narrator, "being dressed in a rich crimson waistcoat and breeches and red feather in his hat, a gold chain around his neck, with a diamond cross hanging to it, a sword in his hand, and two pair of pistols hanging at the end of a silk sling flung over his shoulders according to the fashion of the pirates." Thus he appeared in the last engagement which he fought —that with the *Swallow*—a royal sloop of war. A gallant fight they made of it, those bulldog pirates, for, finding themselves caught in a trap between the man-of-war and the shore, they determined to bear down upon the king's vessel, fire a slapping broadside into her, and then try to get away, trusting to luck and hoping that their enemy might be crippled by their fire.

Captain Roberts himself was the first to fall at the return fire of the *Swallow*; a shot struck him in the neck, and he fell forward across the gun near to which he was standing at the time. A certain fellow named Stevenson, who was at the helm, saw him fall and thought he was wounded. At the lifting of the arm the body rolled over upon the deck, and the man saw that the captain was dead. After their captain's death the pirate crew had no stomach for more fighting; the Black Roger was lowered, and one and all surrendered to justice and the gallows.

Such is a brief and bald account of the most famous of these pirates. But they are only a few of a long list of notables, such as Captain Martel, Captain Charles Vane (who led the gallant Colonel Rhett, of South Carolina, such a wild-goose chase in and out among the sluggish creeks and inlets along the coast), Captain John Rackam, and Captain Anstis, Captains Worley, and Evans, and Philips, and others—twenty or more wild fellows whose very names made ship captains tremble in their shoes in those old times.

And such is that black chapter of history of the past—an evil chapter, lurid with cruelty and suffering, stained with blood and smoke. Yet it is a written chapter, and it must be read. He who chooses may read between the lines of history this great truth: Evil itself is an instrument toward the shaping of good. Therefore the history of evil as well as the history of good should be read, considered, and digested.

The Ruby of Kishmoor

INTRODUCTION

To those who have studied the history of the pirate chieftains who once infested the high seas and preyed so disastrously upon the commerce of the world, the name of Captain Robertson Keitt is well known indeed. But to others, less learned in such matters, it may be said that Captain Keitt's most famous adventure was the capture of the rajah of Kishmoor's great ship *The Sun of the East*, in which was the rajah's favorite queen and a brilliant court of attendants, all of whom were on a pilgrimage to Mecca.

With other treasures there was taken at this time a very famous jewel, which was reputed to be one of the greatest gems in the world. This stone was known as the Ruby of Kishmoor, and the queen, at the time of her capture, wore it upon her forehead as centerpiece of a crown of gold that encircled her brow.

After this famous achievement, Captain Keitt vanished with the Ruby of Kishmoor, and neither was heard of for a long time after.

Shortly before the time of the following story, however, Captain Keitt suddenly appeared in the town of Port Royal, in the island of Jamaica, in company with three of his former confederates in vice —a man named Hunt, who was once his partner, another gallows-bird who had been sailing-master of the pirate ship, and still

121

another villain, a Portuguese who had been first mate of the same wicked craft.

These three worthies took up their lodging at a tavern in the town, where they lived for three or four days without anything particular happening to call attention to them. Then, one night the four were heard to be quarreling with great violence; the next morning Captain Keitt was found dead in the room they had occupied, stabbed in the heart. His pockets had been turned inside out, and the lining of his coat and waistcoat had been ripped in many places. It was supposed at the time that the Ruby of Kishmoor had been the object of his murder, for from that time and until the period of the story about to be told, it was altogether lost sight of.

With a knowledge of these facts, the ingenious reader may be more easily placed in a position to understand the following tale.

JONATHAN RUGG

One never knows what adventurous aspirations may lie hidden beneath the most sedate demeanor.

To have observed Jonathan Rugg, who was a tall, lean, loose-jointed young Quaker of a somewhat forbidding aspect, no one would for a moment have suspected that he concealed beneath so serious an exterior any appetite for romantic adventure.

Nevertheless, finding himself suddenly transported from the quiet of so sober a town as Philadelphia to the tropical enchantment of Kingston, in the island of Jamaica, the street brilliant in the light of a full moon that swung in an opal sky, the warm and luminous darkness filled with the mysteries of a tropical night made merry with the sound of voices, the tinkling of guitars, and an occasional snatch of a song heard from some brightly lighted veranda—seeing and hearing all these things, and with his heart burdened with the odors of a land-breeze, Jonathan Rugg suddenly discovered himself to be overtaken with so strong a desire for excitement, that had the opportunity presented itself he felt himself ready to embrace any adventure with the utmost eagerness, no matter where it would lead him.

Jonathan Rugg had come into this enchanted world as the supercargo, or commerce officer, of the ship *Susanna Hayes* of Philadelphia. He had for several years proved himself so honest and industrious a servant to the merchant house of the worthy Jeremiah Doolittle that that benevolent man had given to his well-deserving clerk this opportunity of gratifying an inclination for foreign travel and of filling a position of trust that would result in his individual profit. The *Susanna Hayes* had entered Kingston Harbor that afternoon, and this was Jonathan's first night spent in those tropical latitudes to where his fancy and his imagination had so often carried him while he stood over his desk filing the accounts of invoices from foreign parts.

It may be finally added that had he at all conceived how soon and to what a degree his sudden inclination for adventure was to be gratified, his romantic desires might have been somewhat dashed if he had known what lay before him.

THE MYSTERIOUS LADY WITH THE SILVER VEIL

As Jonathan Rugg stood thus enjoying the tropical night with no particular purpose in his mind, he suddenly became conscious of the fact that a small wicket in a wooden gate nearby had been opened, and that the eyes of an otherwise concealed person were observing him closely.

He had hardly time to become aware of this observation when the gate itself was opened and there appeared before him in the moonlight the bent and crooked figure of an aged black woman. She was clad in a colorful garment, and was further adorned with a variety of gaudy trimmings vastly suggestive of the tropical world of which she was an inhabitant. Her head was enveloped in the folds of a gigantic and flaming red turban, constructed of an entire pocket-handkerchief.

This woman, first looking this way and then that with an extremely wary and cunning expression, signaled to Jonathan to draw nearer. When he had approached close enough to her, she caught him by the sleeve, and instantly drawing him into the garden beyond, shut and bolted the gate with a quickness and a silence suggestive of the greatest secrecy.

All this had happened so unexpectedly that Jonathan hardly knew what had occurred, until he found himself trapped in the tropical luxuriance of a garden attached to a private dwelling of a very handsome appearance.

For a while the woman who had brought him there gazed at him with a most intense stare. Then suddenly her face broke into an enormous grin. "You be a fine young man," said she. "You come wit' Melina, and Melina take you to pretty lady who want to speak to you."

Then, allowing Jonathan no opportunity either to agree to or to decline the invitation, she took him by the hand and led him toward the large house which overlooked the garden.

Entering this mansion by way of an illuminated veranda, and so coming into a brilliantly lighted hallway beyond, Jonathan saw that he was surrounded by such splendor as it had never before been his good fortune to behold.

Candles of clear wax sparkled like stars in chandeliers of crystal. These, catching the light, glittered in prismatic fragments with all the varied colors of the rainbow. Polished mirrors of a spotless clearness, framed in golden frames and built into the walls, reflected the waxed floors, the rich oriental carpets, and the sumptuous paintings that hung against the ivory-tinted paneling—so that in appearance the beauties of the apartment were continued in bewildering vistas upon every side toward which the beholder directed his gaze.

Asking Jonathan to be seated in this enchanted apartment, the woman who had been his conductor left him for the time being to his own thoughts.

Almost before he had an opportunity to compose himself, the silken curtains at the doorway at the other end of the apartment were suddenly divided, and Jonathan beheld before him a female figure displaying the most exquisite form. She who then entered was clad entirely in white, and was covered from head to foot in the folds of a veil of delicate silver gauze, which, though hiding her face from recognition, nevertheless allowed enough of her beauty to be seen to suggest the extreme loveliness of her appearance. Advancing toward Jonathan and extending to him a delicate hand as white as alabaster, the fingers encircled with many jeweled rings, she addressed him thus:

"Sir, you are undoubtedly surprised to find yourself so unexpectedly introduced into the house of one who is such an entire stranger to you as myself. But though I am unknown to you, I must inform you that I am better acquainted with my visitor, for my agents have been observing you ever since you landed this afternoon at the dock, and they have followed you since then until a little while ago, when you stopped beside my garden gate."

Here the lady paused for a little as though to collect herself, and then continued: "You are doubtless aware that everyone, whether man or woman, is possessed of an enemy. In my own case I must inform you that I have no less than three, who, to accomplish their ends, would gladly sacrifice my life itself to their purposes. At no time am I safe from their evil plans, nor have I anyone," she cried, exhibiting a great emotion, "to whom I may turn in my need. It was this situation that led me to hope to find in you a friend in my perils. Having observed through my agents that you seem honest and strong in character and possess a considerable degree of courage and determination, I desire to impose upon your good nature a trust of which you cannot for a moment suspect the importance. Tell me, are you willing to assist a poor, defenseless female in her hour of trial?"

For a few moments Jonathan stood in silence, for it seemed he was about to enter into an adventure which surpassed any anticipation that he could have formed. He was, besides, of a cautious nature, and was not entirely willing to so quickly agree to involvement in such a mysterious affair.

"Friend," he said at last, "I may tell thee that thy story has so far moved me as to give me every inclination to help thee in thy difficulties, but I must also inform thee that I am a man of caution, having never before entered into any business of this sort. Therefore, before giving any promise that may bind my future actions, I must demand to know what it is that thou hast in mind to require of me."

"Indeed, sir," cried the lady, with great energy and with a new cheerfulness—as though her mind had been relieved of a burden of fear that her companion might decline even a consideration of her request—"indeed, sir, you will find that the trust which I would impose upon you is in appearance no such great matter as my words may have led you to suppose.

"I am possessed of a little trinket which, in the hands of anyone who, like yourself, is a stranger in these parts, would possess no significance, but which, while in my keeping, is filled with infinite menace for me."

Having so spoken, she clapped her hands, and the black woman immediately entered, carrying in her hands a white napkin, which she handed to the lady. The veiled woman unfolded the napkin to reveal a small ivory ball of about the size of a lime. Nodding to the old woman to leave, she handed him the ivory ball. Jonathan took it with curiosity and examined it carefully. It appeared to be very old, and of so deep a yellow as to be almost brown in color. It was covered with strange figures and characters of an oriental sort and appeared to Jonathan to be of Chinese workmanship.

"I must tell you, sir," said the lady, after she had permitted her guest to examine this for a while in silence, "that though this appears to you to be of little worth, it is of extreme value. After all, however, it is nothing but a curiosity that anyone who is interested in such matters might possess. What I have to ask of you is this: Will you be willing to take this and guard it with the utmost care during your stay in these parts, and to return it to me in safety the day before your departure? By doing so you will render me a service which you may neither understand nor comprehend, but which shall make me your debtor for my entire life."

By this time Jonathan had pretty well composed his mind for a reply.

"Friend," said he, "such a matter as this is entirely out of my knowledge of business, which is that of a clerk for a merchant. Nevertheless, I have every inclination to help thee—though I trust thou may have magnified the dangers that beset thee. This appears to me to be a little trifle for such a fuss; nevertheless, I will do as thou dost request. I will keep it in safety and will return it to thee upon this day a week hence—by which time I hope to have discharged my cargo and be ready to continue my voyage to Demerara."

At these words the lady, who had been watching him all the time with eagerness, burst forth into words of such heartfelt gratitude as to entirely overwhelm Jonathan. When she permitted him to depart, the old woman conducted him back through the garden and showed him through the gate where he had entered, and then out into the street.

The Terrific Encounter with the One-Eyed Little Gentleman in Black

Finding himself once more in the open street, Jonathan Rugg stood for a while in the moonlight trying to compose his mind into somewhat of that seriousness that was usual with him. He was aroused from this effort by observing that a little gentleman, clad all in black, had stopped a short distance away and was looking very intently at him. In the brightness of the moonlight Jonathan could see that the little gentleman possessed but a single eye and that he carried a gold-headed cane in his hand. He had hardly time to observe these particulars when the man approached him with every appearance of politeness and cordiality.

"Sir," said he, "surely I am not mistaken in recognizing that you are the commerce officer of the ship *Susanna Hayes*, which arrived this afternoon at this port."

"Indeed," said Jonathan, "thou art right, friend. That is my occupation, and that is where I came from."

"To be sure!" said the little gentleman. "To be sure, to be sure!

The *Susanna Hayes* with a cargo of Indian-corn meal, and from my dear friend Jeremiah Doolittle, of Philadelphia. I know your good master very well—very well indeed. And have you never heard him speak of his friend Mr. Abner Greenway, of Kingston, Jamaica?"

"Why, no," replied Jonathan, "I have no such recollection of the name—nor do I know that any such name hath ever appeared upon our books."

"To be sure, to be sure!" repeated the little gentleman, briskly, and with good nature. "Indeed, my name is not likely to have ever appeared upon his books, for I am not a business associate, but one who in times past was his good friend. There is much I would like to ask about him, and indeed I hoped that you would have been the bearer of a letter from him. I have lodgings a little distance from here, so that if it is not requesting too much of you, maybe you will accompany me there, so that we may talk at our leisure."

"Indeed," said Jonathan—who was of a very easy disposition—"indeed, I shall be very glad to accompany thee to thy lodgings. There is nothing I would like better than to serve any friend of good Jeremiah Doolittle." And with great cordiality the two walked off together.

The one-eyed gentleman in black was so lively in his conversation and had so much to tell him concerning the town that Jonathan was not aware where they were going, until at last he discovered that they had left the residential quarter and had come to the waterfront of the city.

Here, in the midst of a group of buildings that had the appearance of being warehouses for the storage of sugar or molasses, Jonathan's host stopped in front of a tall and gloomy structure, and, opening the door with a key, motioned for him to enter. Jonathan having complied, his new-found friend led the way up a flight of steps, against which Jonathan's feet beat noisily in the darkness. Having ascended two stairways and having reached a landing, the one-eyed man opened a door at the end of the passage and led Jonathan into an apartment, unlighted except for the moonlight, which, coming in through a partly open shutter, lay in a brilliant patch of light upon the floor.

His host having struck a light with a flint and steel, Jonathan, by the illumination of a single candle, discovered himself to be in a bedchamber furnished with a degree of comfort and even elegance, having every appearance of being a bachelor's apartment.

"This," said Jonathan's new acquaintance, "is my lodging-place. And now you will pardon me if I shut these shutters. For a devilish fever of which I am possessed is of such a sort that I must keep the night air out of the room, or else I shall be shaking the bones out of my joints and chattering the teeth out of my head by tomorrow morning."

So saying, he was as good as his word, and not only closed the shutters, but shot the heavy iron bolt into its place. He then asked Jonathan to be seated, and placing before him some superior rum, together with some equally excellent tobacco, they fell into the friendliest conversation imaginable. In the course of their talk, which after a while became most confidential, Jonathan confided to his new friend the circumstances of the adventure into which he had been led by the beautiful stranger.

"Upon my word," said the other, when Jonathan had concluded, "I hope that you may not have been made the victim of some foolish hoax. Let me see what it is the lady has confided to you."

"That I will," replied Jonathan, and he thrust his hand into his pocket and brought forth the ivory ball.

No sooner did the one eye of the little gentleman in black spy the object than a most extraordinary convulsion appeared to seize him.

Mastering his emotion with difficulty as Jonathan replaced the ball in his pocket, he drew a deep breath and wiped the palm of his hand across his forehead as though arousing himself from a dream.

"And you," he said suddenly, "are, as I understand from the way you speak, a Quaker. Do you, then, never carry a weapon even in such a place as this, where at any moment in the dark a Spanish knife may be stuck between your ribs?"

"Why, no," said Jonathan somewhat surprised that such a topic should have been so suddenly introduced into the conversation. "I am a man of peace and not of blood. The people of the Society of Friends never carry weapons either of offense or defense."

As Jonathan concluded his reply, the little gentleman suddenly arose from his chair and moved briskly around to the other side of the room. Watching him with some surprise, Jonathan observed him go to the door and with a single movement shoot the bolt and turn the key. The next instant he turned to Jonathan, suddenly transformed, as though he had dropped a mask from his face. The gossiping and polite little old bachelor was there no longer, but in his stead a man with a face convulsed with some furious and nameless passion.

"That ball!" he cried, in a hoarse and loud voice. "That ivory ball! Give it to me now!"

As he spoke he whipped out from under his shirt a long, sharp Spanish knife that in its every appearance spoke of the most murderous possibilities.

All this Jonathan beheld as one sees such things in a dream, but at the approach of this danger his wits came back to him like a flash of light; leaping to his feet, he lost no time in putting the table between himself and his sudden enemy.

"Indeed, friend," he cried, in a voice penetrated with terror— "indeed, friend, thou hadst best keep thy distance from me, for though I am a man of peace and a shunner of bloodshed, I promise thee that I will not stand still to be murdered without outcry or without endeavoring to defend my life."

"Cry as loud as you please," exclaimed the other, "no one is near this place to hear you. I tell you I am determined to possess that ivory ball, and have it I shall, even if I must cut out your heart to get it!" As he spoke, he grinned with so devilish a distortion of his face as to send the flesh crawling like icy fingers up and down Jonathan's spine.

Nevertheless, mastering his fears, Jonathan spoke up with a pretty good appearance of spirit. "Indeed, friend," he said, "thou may forget that I am a man of twice thy bulk and half thy years. Though thou hast a knife, I am determined to defend myself to the last moment. I am not going to give thee that which thou demandest of me. For thy sake I advise thee to open the door and let me go, or else harm may befall thee."

"Fool," cried the little man, hardly giving him time to end, "do you think that I have time to chatter with you while two villains are lying in wait for me, perhaps at the very door? Blame your own self for your death!" And, gnashing his teeth with an indescribable menace and resting his hand upon the table, he jumped clean across it and upon Jonathan, who, entirely unprepared for such an attack, was flung back against the wall, with an arm as strong as steel clutching his throat and a knife flashing in his eyes with a promise of instant death.

With an instinct to preserve his life, he caught his assailant by the wrist, and bending it away from himself, made a superhuman effort to guard and protect himself. The other, though so much older and smaller, seemed to be composed entirely of fibers of steel, and in his murderous embraces he put forth a strength so extraordinary that for a moment Jonathan felt his heart melt within him with terror for his life. With a cry of despair and anguish he made one stupendous effort for defense, and clapping his heel behind the other's leg and throwing his whole weight forward, he tripped his antagonist backward as he stood. Together they fell upon the floor, locked in the most desperate embrace, and over-turning a chair with a great clatter in their descent—Jonathan upon the top and the little gentleman in black beneath him.

As they struck the floor the little man in black emitted a most piercing and terrible scream, and instantly relaxing his efforts of attack, began beating the floor with the back of his hands and drubbing with his heels upon the rug in which he had become entangled.

Jonathan leaped to his feet, and with bulging eyes and expanding brain and swimming sight stared down upon the other like one turned into stone.

He saw instantly what had occurred—that he had, without so intending, killed a fellow man. The knife, turned away from his own person, had in their fall been plunged into the chest of the other, who now lay quivering in the last moments of death. Even as Jonathan gazed, he saw the one eye of the little gentleman turn upward; he saw the figure stretch itself, shudder, and then become still in death.

THE MOMENTOUS ADVENTURE WITH THE STRANGER WITH THE SILVER EARRINGS

So Jonathan stood stunned and dazed, gazing down upon his victim like a man turned to stone. The dead figure upon the floor at his feet looked at him with a wide, glassy stare, and in the confusion of his mind it appeared to Jonathan that he was indeed a murderer.

What monstrous thing was this that had befallen him who but a moment before had been so entirely innocent of the guilt of blood! How was he, a stranger in a foreign land, to defend himself against an accusing, if mistaken, justice! At these thoughts a dreadful terror gripped at him and a sweat as cold as ice covered his entire body. He must wait for no explanation or defense! He must immediately leave this terrible place, or else, should he be discovered, his doom would certainly be sealed!

At that moment there was suddenly a knock upon the door, sounding so loud and so startling in the silence of the room that every shattered nerve in Jonathan's frame tingled and thrilled in answer to it. He stood petrified, scarcely so much as daring to breathe.

Again there fell the same loud, insistent knock upon the panel, followed by the command, "Open within!"

The wretched Jonathan flung about him a glance of terror and despair, but there was for him no possible escape. He was shut tight in the room with his dead victim, like a rat in a trap. Nothing remained for him but to obey the summons from outside.

With the uncertain movements of an ill-constructed automaton he crossed the room, and stepping very carefully over the body on the floor, and with a hesitation that he could in no degree master, he unlocked, unbolted, and opened the door.

The figure that outlined itself in the light of the candle against the blackness of the passageway outside was of such an unusual and foreign appearance as to fit well into the extraordinary tragedy of which Jonathan was both the victim and the cause.

It was that of a lean, tall man with a thin, yellow face, embellished with a long, black mustache, and having a pair of forbidding, deeply set, and extremely restless black eyes. A crimson handkerchief beneath a laced cocked hat was tied tightly around his head, and a pair of silver earrings, which caught the light of the candle, gleamed and twinkled against the inky darkness of the passageway beyond.

This extraordinary being, without favoring Jonathan with any word of apology for his intrusion, immediately thrust himself forward into the room, and stretching his long, lean, birdlike neck so as to direct his gaze over the intervening table, fixed a gaping and concentrated stare upon the figure lying still and motionless in the center of the room.

"Vat you do dare?" he said, with a guttural and foreign accent. Then, without waiting for a reply, he came forward and knelt down beside the dead man. After thrusting his hand into the lifeless man's coat, he looked up and fixed his penetrating eyes upon Jonathan, who, dazed with despair, still stood like one enchained in the bonds of a nightmare. "He is dead," said the stranger, and Jonathan nodded his head in reply.

"Vy you keel ze man?" inquired the tall stranger.

"Indeed," cried Jonathan, finding a voice at last, but one so hoarse that he could hardly recognize it for his own, "I know not what to make of the affair. But, I do assure thee, friend, that I am entirely innocent of what thou seest!"

The stranger still kept his piercing gaze fixed upon Jonathan, who, feeling that something further was demanded of him, continued: "I am, indeed, a victim of a most extraordinary adventure. This evening, coming as a stranger to this country, I was introduced into the house of a beautiful female, who bestowed upon me a task both insignificant and absurd. Behold this little ivory ball," said he, drawing the globe from his pocket and displaying it between his thumb and finger. "It is this that appears to have brought all this disaster upon me."

He continued his explanations no further, for at the sight of the ivory ball, the stranger quickly arose from his kneeling posture and stared wildly at Jonathan. His eyes dilated like those of a cat, and the breath expelled itself from his bosom so violently that it appeared as though it might never return. As Jonathan, much amazed at his expression, replaced the ball in his pocket, the other man moved suddenly, as if from an electric shock. A sudden light flamed into his eyes; his face grew as red as blood, and he clapped his hands to his pocket with a quick and violent motion. "Ze ball!" he cried in a hoarse and screeching voice. "Ze ball! Give me ze ball!" And in the next instant Jonathan saw the round and shining nozzle of a pistol pointed directly against his forehead.

For a moment he stood as though frozen; and then, in the mortal peril that faced him, he uttered a roar that sounded in his own ears like the outcry of a wild beast. He flung himself bodily upon the other man with the violence and the fury of a madman.

The stranger drew the trigger and the powder flashed. He dropped the weapon, clattering, and in an instant tried to draw another from his other pocket. Before he could direct his aim, however, Jonathan had caught him by both wrists, and bending his hand backward, prevented the chance of any shot hitting him. Then followed a ferocious struggle—the stranger trying to free his hand, and Jonathan striving with all the energy of despair to prevent him from achieving his murderous goal.

In the struggle Jonathan was thrust against the edge of the table. He felt as though his back were breaking and became conscious that in such a situation he could hope to defend himself only a few moments longer. The stranger's face was pressed close to his own. His hot breath, strong with the odor of garlic, fanned Jonathan's cheek, while his lips, twisted into a ferocious and bestial grin, displayed his sharp teeth shining in the candlelight.

"Give me ze ball!" he said, in a harsh and furious whisper.

At that moment there rang in Jonathan's ears the sudden and astounding sound of a pistol shot, and for a moment he wondered whether he had received a mortal wound without being aware of it. Then suddenly he saw an amazing transformation take place in the face thrust so close to his own: the eyes winked rapidly several times and then rolled upward and inward; the jaws opened into a dreadful and cavernous yawn; the pistol fell with a clatter to the floor; and the next moment the muscles, so rigid but an instant before, became limp and lifeless. The joints collapsed, and the entire man fell into a heap across the dead figure stretched out on the floor; at the same time a strong-smelling and blinding cloud of gunpowder smoke filled the entire apartment. For a few moments the hands twitched convulsively; the neck stretched itself to an abominable length; the long, lean legs slowly and gradually relaxed, and every fiber of the body collapsed into death. A spot of blood appeared and grew upon the collar at the throat, and in the same degree the color left the face, leaving it a dull and leaden color.

All these terrible changes of aspect Jonathan stood watching in motionless and riveted attention, as though they were to him matters of the utmost importance. Only when the last flicker of life had departed from his second victim did he lift his gaze from this terrible scene to stare about him, this way and that, his eyes blinded and his breath stifled by the thick cloud of sulphurous smoke that obscured the objects about him.

The Unexpected Encounter with the Sea-Captain with the Broken Nose

Then at last Jonathan aroused himself. Mechanically he picked up his hat, which had fallen upon the floor in the first encounter, and, brushing away the dust with the cuff of his coat-sleeve with care, he adjusted the beaver cap upon his head. Then turning, still stupefied as with the fumes of some powerful drug, he prepared to quit the scene of the tragic terrors that had unexpectedly fallen upon him.

But before he could put his plan into execution, his ears were startled by the sound of loud and hurried footsteps, which, coming from below, ascended the stairs with great clatter and speed. At the landing these footsteps paused for a while, and then approached with more caution and deliberation toward the room where the double tragedy had been enacted.

All this while Jonathan made no attempt to escape, but stood passively, submissive to what might occur. He felt himself the victim of circumstances over which he himself had no control. Gazing at the partly opened door, he waited for whatever adventure might next befall him. Once again the footsteps paused, this time at the very threshold; then the door was slowly pushed open from outside.

As Jonathan gazed at the opening, there was revealed to his view the strong and robust figure of one who was evidently of a seafaring habit. From the gold braid on his hat, the seals dangling from the ribbon of his pocket watch, and a certain fussiness of manner, he was evidently a person of some importance in his profession. He was of a strong and powerful build, with a head set close to his shoulders, and a round, short, bull neck. He wore a black neckerchief, loosely tied into a knot, and a red waistcoat elaborately trimmed with gold braid; a leather belt with a brass buckle and hanger, and huge sea-boots, completed a costume suggestive of his occupation. His face was round and broad, like that of a cat, of a complexion stained by constant exposure to the sun and wind to a color of newly polished mahogany. But a face which otherwise might have been humorous in this case was rendered repulsive by the fact that his nose had been broken so flat to his face that all that remained to distinguish that feature were two circular orifices where the nostrils should have been. His eyes were by no means as sinister as the rest of his face, being of a light-gray color and very lively—even good-natured in the merry restlessness of their glance —although they were almost hidden beneath a black bush of overhanging eyebrows. When he spoke, his voice was so deep and resonant that it was as though it came from a barrel rather than from the chest of a human being.

"How now, my hearty!" he cried, in tones so loud that they seemed to stun the tensely drawn drums of Jonathan's ears. "How now, my hearty! What's to-do here? Who is shooting pistols at this hour of the night?" Then catching sight of the figures lying in a huddle upon the floor, his great thick lips parted into a gape of wonder and his gray eyes rolled in his head like two balls, so that, with his flat face and the round holes of his nostrils, he presented an appearance which under other circumstances would have been both laughable and grotesque.

"By the blood!" cried he. "To be sure, it is murder that has happened here."

"Not murder!" cried Jonathan, in a shrill and panting voice. "Not murder! It was all an accident, and I am as innocent as a baby."

The newcomer looked at him, and then at the two figures on the floor, and then back at him again, with eyes at once questioning and cunning. Then his face broke into a grin. "Accident!" he said. "By the blood! 'Tis a strange accident indeed that lays two men by the heels and lets the third go without a scratch!" He then came forward into the room; taking the last victim of Jonathan's adventure by the arm, with as little care as if he was handling a sack of grain, he dragged the limp and helpless figure from where it lay to the floor beside the first victim. Then lifting the lighted candle, he bent over the two bodies, holding the illumination close to the remains first of one and then of the other. He looked at them very carefully for a long while with the closest and most intense scrutiny and in perfect silence. "They are both as dead," said he, "as Davy Jones. And, whoever you be, I protest you have done your business in the most complete way that I ever saw in all of my life."

"Indeed," cried Jonathan, in the same shrill and panting voice, "it was they themselves who did it. First one of them attacked me and then the other, and I did but try to keep them from murdering me. This one fell on his knife, and that one shot himself in his efforts to destroy me."

"That," said the seaman, "you may very well tell to a dry-lander, and maybe he will believe you, but you cannot so easily pull the wool over the eyes of Captain Benny Willitts. And what, if I may be so bold to ask you, was the reason for their attacking so harmless a man as you proclaim yourself to be?"

"That I do not know," cried Jonathan, "but I am entirely willing to tell thee all the circumstances. Thou must know that I am a member of the Society of Friends. This day I landed here in Kingston and met a young woman of very fine appearance, who entrusted me with this little ivory ball, which she requested me to keep for her a few days. The sight of this ball—in which I can detect nothing that could be likely to arouse any feelings of violence—appears to have driven these two men entirely mad, so that they instantly made the most ferocious and murderous assault upon me. See! Wouldst thou have believed that so small a thing as this would have caused so much trouble?" And as he spoke he held up to the gaze of the other man the cause of the recent tragic events.

No sooner had Captain Willitts's eyes viewed the ball than a change passed over his face. The color appeared to grow dull and yellow in his ruddy cheeks, his fat lips dropped apart, and his eyes glared with a fixed and glassy stare. He rose to his feet and, still with an expression of astonishment and wonder on his face, gazed first at Jonathan and then at the ivory ball in his hands, as though he were deprived of both reason and speech. At last, as Jonathan slipped the trifle back in his pocket again, the mariner slowly recovered himself, though with a major effort, and drew a deep and profound breath, as if from the very bottom of his lungs. With the corner of his black silk neckerchief he wiped his brow, upon which the sweat appeared to have gathered.

"Well, messmate," he said at last, with a sudden change of tone, "you have indeed had a most wonderful adventure." Then, with another deep breath: "Well, by the blood! I may tell you plainly that I am no poor hand at the reading of faces. Well, I think you to be honest, and I am inclined to believe every word you tell me. By the blood! I am sorry for you, and am inclined to help you out of your scrape.

"The first thing to do," he continued, "is to get rid of these here two dead men, and that is a task, I believe, we shall have no trouble in handling. One of them we will wrap up in the carpet here, and t'other we can roll in that bed-curtain. You shall carry the one and I the other. The harbor being at no great distance, we can easily bring them there and tumble them overboard, and no one will be the wiser of what has happened. For your own safety, as you may easily see, you can hardly go away and leave these objects here to be found by the first comer and to arise up in evidence against you."

This reasoning, in Jonathan's present bewildered state, appeared to him to be so extremely just that he raised not the least objection to it. So each of the two voiceless victims of the evening's occurrences was wrapped into a bundle that on its surface was neither revealing nor terrible.

Then Jonathan, shouldering his rug containing the little gentleman in black, and the sea-captain, doing the like for the other, made their way down the stairs through the darkness and out into the street. Here the sea-captain became the conductor of the expedition and led the way down an alley—both men now and then stopping to rest, for both burdens were too heavy and clumsy to carry with ease. They came at last upon an open wharf extending a good distance out into the harbor. The captain led the way, and, Jonathan following, they made their way out along the wharf or pier, stumbling now and then over loose boards, until they came at last to where the water was of a sufficient depth for their purpose. Here the captain, bending his shoulders, shot his burden out into the dark, mysterious waters, and Jonathan, following his example, did the same. Each body sank with a leaden splash into the water; and the casings which swathed them becoming loosened, the rug and the curtain rose to the surface and drifted slowly away with the tide.

As Jonathan stood gazing at the disappearance of the last evidence of his two unintended murders, he suddenly felt a pair of arms of enormous strength flung around him from behind. In their embrace his elbows were instantly pinned tight to his side, and he stood for a moment helpless and astounded, while the voice of the sea-captain rumbling in his ear exclaimed: "Ye bloody, murdering Quaker—I'll have that ivory ball, or I'll have your life!"

These words produced upon Jonathan the effect of having cold water suddenly flung over him. He began instantly to struggle to free himself, with a frantic and vehement violence born of terror and despair. So great were his efforts that more than once he had nearly torn himself free, but still the powerful arms of his captor held him as in a vise of iron. Meantime Jonathan's assailant made frequent though ineffectual attempts to thrust a hand into the pocket where the ivory ball was hidden, swearing under his breath with a terrifying and monstrous string of oaths. At last, finding himself stopped in every such attempt, and losing all patience at the struggles of his victim, he tried to lift Jonathan off his feet as though to dash him bodily to the ground. In this he would surely have succeeded had he not caught his heel upon one of the loose boards. Instantly they both fell violently to the ground, the captain beneath and Jonathan above him, though still encircled in his iron embrace. As they fell Jonathan felt the back of his head strike violently upon the flat face of the other, and he heard the captain's skull sound with a terrific crack, like that of a breaking egg, upon some wooden post against which he must have struck. In their frantic struggles they had approached very near to the edge of the wharf, so that the next instant, with an enormous and thunderous splash, Jonathan found himself plunged into the waters of the harbor, and the arms of his assailant loosened from around his body.

The shock of the water brought him instantly to his senses, and being a fairly good swimmer, he had no difficulty in reaching and clutching the cross-piece of a wooden ladder that, coated with slimy sea-moss, led from the water level to the wharf above.

After reaching the safety of dry land once more, Jonathan gazed about him as though to judge from where the next attack might come from. But he stood entirely alone upon the dock—not another living soul was in sight. The surface of the water exhibited some commotion as though disturbed by something struggling beneath, but the sea-captain, who had undoubtedly been stunned by the tremendous crack upon his head, never arose again out of the element that had engulfed him.

The moonlight shone with a splendid illumination, and, except for certain remote noises from the distant town, not a sound broke the silence and the peacefulness of the balmy tropical night. The calm water, lit by the moonlight, lapped against the wharf. All the world was calm, serene, and enveloped in a profound rest.

Jonathan stood for a little while looking up at the round and brilliant globe of light floating in the sky above his head. Then suddenly arousing himself to a renewed realization of what had occurred, he turned and ran like one possessed from the scene of this third and final catastrophe.

THE CONCLUSION OF THE ADVENTURE WITH
THE LADY IN THE SILVER VEIL

A few minutes later, Jonathan, dripping wet, stood at the gate of the garden, beating and kicking it with fury that he could not control. He was aware that the entire neighborhood was becoming aroused, that lights were moving and that loud voices of inquiry were sounding in neighboring houses.

At last, in answer to his vehement blows, a pair of eyes appeared at the small grated window. The next instant the gate was opened very hastily and the familiar old woman appeared. She caught Jonathan by the sleeve of his coat and drew him quickly into the garden.

"What you doing?" she cried. "You wake d' whole town." Then, observing his dripping garments: "You been in d' water. You catch d' fever and shake till you die."

"Thy mistress!" cried Jonathan, almost sobbing in the excess of his emotion. "Take me to her now, or I may not prevent myself from going entirely mad!"

When Jonathan again stood in the presence of the lady, he found her clad in loose attire infinitely becoming to her graceful figure, and once again covered with a veil of silver gauze.

"Friend," he cried, vehemently, approaching her and holding out toward her the little ivory ball, "take again this which thou gavest me. It has brought death to three men, and I know not what horrible fate may befall me if I keep it longer in my possession."

"What is it you say?" cried she, in a piercing voice. "Did you say it caused the death of three men? Quick! Tell me what has happened, for I feel that you bring me news of safety and release from all my dangers."

"I know not what thou meanest," cried Jonathan, still panting with agitation. "But this I do know: that when I went away from thee I departed an innocent man, and now I come back to thee burdened with the weight of three lives, which, though I be innocent, I have been instrumental in taking."

"Explain," exclaimed the lady, tapping the floor with her foot. "Explain! Explain! Explain!"

"That I will," cried Jonathan, "and as soon as I am able. When I left thee and went out into the street, I was approached by a little gentleman clad in black."

"Indeed!" cried the lady. "And had he but one eye, and did he carry a gold-headed cane?"

"Exactly," said Jonathan, "and he claimed acquaintance with my friend Jeremiah Doolittle."

"He never knew him," cried the lady, "and I must tell you that he was a villain named Hunt, who at one time was the partner of the pirate Keitt. He it was who plunged a deadly knife into his captain's bosom, and so murdered him one night in Port Royal. He himself or his agents must have been watching my gate when you left."

"I know not how that may be," said Jonathan, "but he took me to his apartment, and there, obtaining a knowledge of the object thou didst burden me with, he demanded it of me, and upon my refusing to deliver it to him, he attacked me with a dagger. In my efforts to protect my life I accidently caused him to plunge the knife into his own chest and to kill himself."

"And what then?" cried the lady, nearly overcome by her emotions.

"Then," said Jonathan, "there came a strange man—a foreigner —who assaulted me with a pistol, with every intention of murdering me and thus obtaining possession of that same object."

"And did he," exclaimed the lady, "have a long, black mustache, and did he have silver earrings in his ears?"

"Yes," said Jonathan, "he did."

"That," cried the lady, "could have been none other than the Portuguese mate of Captain Keitt's ship, *The Bloody Hand*, who must have been spying upon Hunt! Tell me what happened next!"

"He would have taken my life," said Jonathan, "but in the struggle that followed he shot himself accidentally with his own pistol and died at my very feet. I do not know what would have happened to me if a sea-captain had not come and offered his assistance."

"A sea-captain!" she exclaimed. "And had he a flat face and a broken nose?"

"Indeed he had," replied Jonathan.

"That," said the lady, "must have been Captain Keitt's sailing-master, Captain Willitts. He was probably spying upon the Portuguese."

"He convinced me," said Jonathan, "to carry the two bodies down to the wharf. Having brought me there—where, I suppose, he thought no one could interfere—he assaulted me and tried to take the ivory ball away from me. In my efforts to escape we both fell into the water, and he, striking his head upon the edge of the wharf, was first stunned and then drowned."

"Thank God!" cried the lady with much emotion, as she clasped her jeweled hands together. "At last I am free of those who have for so long persecuted me and threatened my life! You have not asked to see my face; I will now show it to you. Before now I have been obliged to keep it concealed; for, recognizing me, my enemies surely would have slain me."

As she spoke she drew aside her veil, and revealed to Jonathan a face of the most extraordinary and striking beauty. Her dark and luminous eyes were set beneath exquisitely arched brows. Her forehead was like lustrous ivory, and her lips like rose leaves. Her hair, which was as soft as the finest silk, was fastened in ravishing masses.

"I am," said she, "the daughter of that unfortunate Captain Keitt, who, though weak and a pirate, was not so wicked, I would have you know, as he has been painted. He would undoubtedly have been an honest man had he not been led astray by the villain Hunt, who so nearly brought on your own destruction. He returned to this island before his death and made me the sole heir of the

The Ruby of Kishmoor

The Ruby of Kishmoor

great fortune which he had gathered—perhaps not by the most honest means—in the waters of the Indian Ocean. But the greatest treasure of all the fortune left to me was a single jewel, which you yourself have just now defended with a courage and a fidelity that I cannot praise enough. It is that priceless gem known as the Ruby of Kishmoor. I will show it to you."

She took the little ivory ball in her hand, and with a turn of her beautiful wrists unscrewed a lid so nicely and cunningly adjusted that no eye could have detected where it was joined to the parent globe. Within was a piece of raw silk containing a red stone of about the size of a pigeon's egg, which glowed and flamed with such brilliance as to dazzle even Jonathan's inexperienced eyes. Indeed, he did not need to be informed of the priceless value of the treasure which he beheld in the rosy palm extended toward him. How long he gazed at this extraordinary jewel he did not know, but he was aroused from his concentration by the sound of the lady's voice addressing him.

"The three villains," she said, "who have this day met their just deserts in violent bloody deaths, had by an accident obtained knowledge that this jewel was in my possession. Since then my life has hung upon a thread, and every step that I have taken has been watched by these cruel and relentless enemies. From the mortal dangers of their plottings you have saved me, exhibiting a courage and a determination that cannot be sufficiently applauded. In this you have earned my deepest admiration and regard. I would rather," she cried, "entrust my life and my happiness to you than into the keeping of any man whom I have ever known. I cannot hope to reward you in such a way as to compensate you for the perils into which my needs have thrust you, but yet"—and here she hesitated as though seeking words in which to express herself— "but yet, if you are willing to accept this jewel and all of the fortune that belongs to me, together with the person of poor Evelina

Keitt herself, not only the stone and the wealth, but the woman also, is yours."

Jonathan was so struck at her words that he knew not what reply to make. "Friend," he said at last, "I thank thee extremely for thy offer, and though I would not be ungracious, I must tell thee that as to the stone itself and the fortune I have no inclination to receive either the one or the other. Each is the fruit of theft and murder. The jewel I have myself beheld three times stained with the blood of my fellow men, so that it now has so little value in my sight that I would not give a peppercorn to possess it. Indeed, there is no inducement in the world that could persuade me to accept it. As to the rest of thy generous offer, I have only to say that I am, four months from now, to be married to a fine young woman of Kensington, in Pennsylvania, by the name of Martha Dobbs—and therefore I am not at liberty to consider my inclinations in any other direction."

Having so spoken, Jonathan bowed with such ease as his stiff and awkward joints might allow, and then withdrew from the presence of the charmer, who, with blushing cheeks and with eyes averted, made no attempt to stop him.

So ended the only important adventure that ever happened to Jonathan Rugg in all his life. For, thereafter, he contented himself with such excitement as his mercantile profession and his extremely peaceful existence might allow.

EPILOGUE

In conclusion it may be said that when the worthy Jonathan Rugg was married to Martha Dobbs the following year, some mysterious friend presented to the bride a rope of pearls of such considerable value that, when they were exchanged for money, Jonathan was enabled to enter into partnership with his former patron, the worthy Jeremiah Doolittle, and that having made such a beginning, he arose to become one of the leading merchants of his native town of Philadelphia.

Captain Scarfield

I

Eleazer Cooper, or Captain Cooper, as was his better-known title in Philadelphia, was a prominent member of the Society of Friends. He was an appointed overseer of the regular Quaker meeting and was even a speaker on special occasions. When at home from one of his many voyages he never failed to occupy his seat in the meeting both on First Day and Fifth Day, and he was regarded by his fellow townspeople as a model of business integrity and of domestic responsibility.

More important to this history, however, is the fact that Captain Cooper was one of those trading skippers who carried their own merchandise in their own vessels which they sailed themselves, and on whose decks they did their own bartering. His vessel was a swift, large schooner, the *Eliza Cooper of Philadelphia*, named for his wife. His cruising grounds were the West Indies islands, and his merchandise was flour and cornmeal ground at the Brandywine Mills at Wilmington, Delaware.

During the War of 1812 he had earned an extraordinary fortune in this trading; for flour and cornmeal sold at fabulous prices in the French, Spanish, Dutch, and Danish islands, which were cut off from the rest of the world by the British blockade.

The running of this blockade was one of the most hazardous maritime ventures possible, but Captain Cooper had met with such success, and had sold his merchandise at such a profit that, at the end of the war, he found that he had become one of the wealthiest merchants of his native city.

It was known at one time that his balance in the Mechanics' Bank was greater than that of any other individual depositor, and it was said of him that he had once deposited in the bank a chest of foreign silver coin, the exchanged value of which, when translated into American currency, was almost forty-two thousand dollars—a great sum of money in those days.

In person, Captain Cooper was tall and angular of frame. His face was thin and severe, wearing continually an unsmiling, mask-like expression of unruffled seriousness. His manner was dry and reserved, and his conduct and life were measured to the most absolute accord with the teachings of his religious belief.

He lived in an old-fashioned house on Front Street below Spruce —as pleasant, cheerful a house as ever a trading captain could return to. At the back of the house a lawn sloped steeply down toward the river. To the south stood the wharf and storehouses; to the north an orchard and kitchen garden abundantly bloomed. Two large chestnut trees sheltered the porch and the little space of lawn, and when you sat under them in the shade you looked down the slope between two rows of box bushes directly across the shining river to the Jersey shore.

At the time of this story—that is, about the year 1820—this property had increased greatly in value, but it was the old home of the Coopers, as Eleazer Cooper was entirely rich enough to indulge his fancy in such matters. Since he chose to live in the same house where his father and his grandfather had dwelt before him, he quietly refused all offers for the purchase of the lot of ground— though it was now worth five or six times its former value.

As was said, it was a cheerful, pleasant home, impressing you when you entered it with a feeling of complete cleanliness—a cleanliness that greeted you in the shining brass door-knocker, that entertained you in the sitting room with its stiff, leather-covered furniture, whose brass-headed tacks sparkled like so many stars—a cleanliness that bid you farewell in the spotless stretch of sand-sprinkled hallway, the wooden floor of which was worn into knobs around the nail heads by the countless scourings and scrubbings to which it had been subjected and which left behind them a faint, fragrant odor of soap and warm water.

Eleazer Cooper and his wife were childless, but one resident made the great, silent, shady house bright with life. Lucinda Fairbanks, a niece of Captain Cooper's by his only sister, was a handsome, sprightly girl of eighteen or twenty, and a great favorite in the Quaker society of the city.

It remains only to introduce the final and, perhaps, the most important character of the story—Lieutenant James Mainwaring. During the past twelve months or so he had been a frequent visitor at the Cooper house. At this time he was a broad-shouldered, red-cheeked, stalwart fellow of twenty-six or twenty-eight. He was a great social favorite and possessed the added romantic interest of having been aboard the *Constitution* when she fought the *Guerriere,* and of having, with his own hands, touched the match that fired the first gun of that great battle.

Mainwaring's mother and Eliza Cooper had always been intimate friends, and the coming and going of the young man during his leave of absence were looked upon in the house as quite normal occurrences. Half a dozen times a week he would drop in to do some little chore for the ladies, or, if Captain Cooper was at home, to smoke a pipe of tobacco with him, to sip a dram of his famous old Jamaica rum, or to play a game of checkers in the evening. It is not likely that either of the older people was the least aware of the real cause of his visits; still less did they suspect that any words of sentiment had passed between the young people.

The truth was that Mainwaring and the young lady were very much in love. It was a love that they were obliged to keep secret, for not only had Eleazer Cooper professed the strictest sort of objection against the recent war—an objection so strong as to render it unlikely that one of so military a profession as Mainwaring practiced could hope for his consent for marriage—but Lucinda could not have married one not a member of the Society of Friends without losing her own birthright membership. She herself might not attach much weight to such a loss of membership in the Society, but her fear of, and her respect for, her uncle led her to walk very closely in her path of duty in this area. So, she and Mainwaring met as they could—secretly—and the stolen moments were very sweet. With equal secrecy Lucinda had sat for a miniature portrait by Mrs. Gregory, and this miniature, set in a gold medallion, Mainwaring, with a mild, sentimental pleasure, wore hung around his neck and beneath his shirt, next his heart.

In the month of April of the year 1820, Mainwaring received orders to report to Washington. During the preceding autumn the West Indies pirates, and notably Captain Jack Scarfield, had been more than usually active, and the loss of the ship *Marblehead* (which, sailing from Charleston, South Carolina, was never heard of again) was attributed to them. Two other coasting vessels off the coast of Georgia had been looted and burned by Scarfield, and the government had at last acknowledged the need for measures to rid the West Indies waters of these pests.

Mainwaring received orders to take command of the *Yankee*, a swift, light-draft, heavily armed brig of war, and to cruise about the Bahama Islands and to capture and destroy all the pirates' vessels he could discover there.

On his way from Washington to New York, where the *Yankee* was then waiting orders, Mainwaring stopped in Philadelphia to bid goodbye to his many friends in that city. He called at the old Cooper house. It was on a Sunday afternoon. The spring was early and the weather extremely pleasant that day, being filled with a summerlike warmth. The apple trees were already in full bloom and filled the air with their fragrance. Everywhere there seemed to be the hum of bees, and the drowsy, warm sunshine was delightful.

At that time Eleazer was just home from an unusually successful voyage to Antigua. Mainwaring found the family sitting under one of the still leafless chestnut trees, Captain Cooper smoking his long clay pipe and lazily looking over a copy of the *National Gazette*. Eleazer listened with much interest to what Mainwaring had to say of his proposed cruise. He himself knew a great deal about the pirates, and unbending from his normal stiff attitude, he began telling what he knew, particularly of Captain Scarfield—in whom he appeared to take an extraordinary interest.

To Mainwaring's surprise, the old Quaker became a defender of the pirates, protesting that the wickedness of the accused was enormously exaggerated. He declared that he knew some of the freebooters very well and that at the most they were poor, misdirected wretches who had slid into their evil ways from having been tempted by the government authorities to enter into privateering in the days of the recent war. He conceded that Captain Scarfield had done many cruel and wicked deeds but that he had also performed many kind and benevolent actions: the world made no note of these, but took care only to condemn the evil that had been done. He acknowledged that it was true that the pirate had allowed his crew to cast lots for the wife and the daughter of the skipper of the *Northern Rose*; but none of his accusers told how, at the risk of his own life and the lives of all his crew, he had given aid to the schooner *Halifax*, found adrift with all hands afflicted by with yellow fever. There was no defender of his actions to tell how he and

his crew of pirates had sailed the stricken vessel almost into the rescuing waters of Kingston Harbor. Eleazer confessed that he could not deny that when Scarfield had tied the skipper of the *Baltimore Belle* naked to the foremast of his own brig he had permitted his crew of cutthroats (who were drunk at the time) to throw bottles at the helpless captive, who died that night of the wounds he had received. For this he was very justly condemned; but who was there to praise him when he had, at the risk of his life and in the face of the authorities, carried a cargo of provisions which he himself had purchased at Tampa Bay to the island of Bella Vista after the great hurricane of 1818? In this notable adventure he had barely escaped, after two days' chase, the British frigate *Ceres*, whose captain, had a capture been made, would instantly have hung the unfortunate man to the yardarm in spite of the benevolent mission in which he was involved.

In all this Eleazer seemed to be conducting a case for the "defendant." As he talked he became louder and more animated. The light went out in his pipe, and a ruddy spot appeared in both of his thin cheeks. Mainwaring sat wondering how the severely peaceful Quaker preacher could defend so notoriously bloody and cruel a cutthroat pirate as Captain Jack Scarfield. The warm and innocent surroundings, the old brick house looking down upon them, the odor of apple blossoms and the hum of bees seemed to make it all the more strange. And still the elderly Quaker skipper talked on and on with hardly an interruption, till the warm sun slanted to the west and the day began to decline.

That evening Mainwaring stayed for tea, and when he parted from Lucinda Fairbanks it was after nightfall, with a clear, round moon shining in the milky sky and an unreal radiance covering the old house, the blooming apple trees, the sloping lawn, and the shining river beyond. He begged his sweetheart to let him tell her uncle and aunt of their love and to ask the old man's consent to it, but she would not permit him to do so. They were so happy as they were. Who knew if her uncle might forbid their fondness? Would he not wait a little longer? Maybe it would all come out right after a while. She was so tender, so tearful at the nearness of their parting that he had not the heart to insist. At the same time it was with a feeling almost of despair that he realized that he must now be gone—maybe for the space of two years—without in all that time possessing the right to call her his before the world.

When he said farewell to the older people it was with a feeling of bitter disappointment. He still felt the pressure of her cheeks and lips upon his face. But what were such hidden moments compared to what might, perhaps, be his—the right of calling her his own when he was far away and upon the distant sea? And, besides, he felt like a coward who had shirked his duty.

But he was very much in love. The next morning appeared in a drizzle of rain that followed the beautiful warmth of the day before. He had the coach all to himself, and in the damp and leathery solitude he drew out the little oval picture from beneath his shirt-frill and looked long and with a fond and foolish joy at the innocent face, the blue eyes, the red, smiling lips depicted upon the satin-like, ivory surface.

II

For the better part of five months Mainwaring cruised about in the waters surrounding the Bahama Islands. In that time he dispersed a dozen nests of pirates. He destroyed no less than fifteen piratical crafts of all sizes, from a large half-decked whaleboat to a three-hundred-ton barkentine. The name of the *Yankee* became a terror to every sea-wolf in the western tropics, and the waters of the Bahama Islands became swept almost clean of the bloody wretches who had so lately infested it.

But the one freebooter of all others whom he sought—Captain Jack Scarfield—seemed to evade him like a shadow, to slip through his fingers like magic. Twice he came almost within touch of the famous marauder, both times in the ominous wrecks that the pirate captain had left behind him. The first of these was the water-logged remains of a burned and still smoking wreck that he found adrift in the great Bahama Channel. It was the *Water Witch of Salem,* but he did not learn her tragic story until, two weeks later, he discovered a part of her crew at Port Maria, on the northern coast of Jamaica. It was, indeed, a dreadful story to which he listened. The castaways said that they of all the vessel's crew had been spared so that they might tell the commander of the *Yankee,* should they meet him, that he might keep what he found, with Captain Scarfield's compliments, who served it up to him hot cooked.

Lieutenant James Mainwaring twice came almost within touch
of Captain Jack Scarfield, both times finding only
the smoking remains of attacked ships.

Three weeks later he rescued what remained of the crew of the shattered, bloody hulk of the *Baltimore Belle*, eight of whose crew, headed by the captain, had been tied hand and foot and heaved overboard. Again, there was a message from Captain Scarfield to the commander of the *Yankee* that he might season what he found to suit his own taste.

Mainwaring was of a sturdy disposition, with a fiery temper. He swore passionately that either he or John Scarfield would have to leave the earth.

He had little suspicion of how soon was to occur the dreadful realization of his angry prophecy.

At that time one of the chief meeting-places of the pirates was the little island of San José, one of the southernmost of the Bahama group. Here, in the days before the coming of the *Yankee*, they usually put in to clean their vessels and to take in a fresh supply of provisions, gunpowder, and rum, before renewing their attacks upon the peaceful commerce circulating up and down the islands, or through the wide stretches of the Bahama Channel.

Mainwaring had made several raids upon this nest of freebooters. He had already made two notable captures, and it was here he hoped eventually to capture Captain Scarfield himself.

A brief description of this one-time notorious nest of freebooters might not be out of place. It consisted of a little settlement of those mud-smeared houses such as you find through the West Indies. There were only three houses of a better sort, built of wood. One of these was a storehouse, another was a rum shop, and a third a house in which dwelt a woman who was reputed to be a sort of secret wife of Captain Scarfield. The population consisted of a varied accumulation of black sailors, Yankee traders, poor Spaniards, and a multitude of women and children of all races. The settlement stood in a bend of the beach forming a small harbor and offering a good anchorage for small vessels. The houses, or cabins,

were surrounded by clusters of cocoa-palms and growths of ba-
nanas; a long curve of white beach, sheltered from the large Atlantic waves that exploded upon an outer bar, was drawn like a neck-
lace around the semicircle of emerald-green water.

Such was the famous pirates' settlement of San José—a paradise
of nature and a hell of human depravity and wickedness—and it
was to this spot that Mainwaring paid another visit a few days after
rescuing the crew of the *Baltimore Belle* from her shattered and
sinking wreck.

As the little bay with its fringe of palms and its cluster of mud-
and-straw huts opened up to view, Mainwaring discovered a vessel
lying at anchor in the harbor. It was a large and well-rigged
schooner with 250 or 300 tons' cargo. As the *Yankee* rounded to
under the stern of the stranger and dropped anchor in such a position as to bring her broadside battery to bear should the occasion
require, Mainwaring set his spyglass to his eye to read the name he
could distinguish beneath the overhang of her stern. It is impossible to describe his infinite surprise when he read, *Eliza Cooper of
Philadelphia.*

He could not believe the evidence of his senses. Certainly this
stinkpool of thieves was the last place in the world he would have
expected to have encountered Eleazer Cooper.

He ordered out the gig and had himself immediately rowed over
to the schooner. Whatever lingering doubts he might have had
about the identity of the vessel were quickly dispelled when he saw
Captain Cooper himself standing at the gangway to meet him. The
emotionless face of the Friend showed neither surprise nor confusion at what must have been to him a most unexpected encounter.

But when he stepped upon the deck of the *Eliza Cooper* and
looked about him, Mainwaring could hardly believe the evidence of
his senses at the transformation that he beheld. Upon the main
deck were eight twelve-pound cannons neatly covered with canvas

sheets; in the bow a Long Tom, also snugly stowed away and covered, directed a veiled and muzzled snout out over the ship-stem's stout projecting pole.

It was entirely impossible for Mainwaring to conceal his astonishment at so unexpected a sight, and whether or not his own thoughts lent color to his imagination, it seemed to him that Eleazer Cooper concealed under his stern expression a degree of confusion.

After Captain Cooper had led the way into the cabin and he and the younger man were seated over a pipe of tobacco and the usual bottle of fine old Jamaica rum, Mainwaring made no attempt to refrain from questioning him about the reason for this dreadful transformation.

"I am a man of peace, James Mainwaring," Eleazer replied, "but there are men of blood in these waters, and an appearance of great strength is of use to protect the innocent from the wicked. If I remained in appearance the peaceful trader I really am, how long dost thou suppose I could remain unassailed in this place?"

It occurred to Mainwaring that the powerful weaponry he had seen was rather extreme to be used merely as a preventive. He smoked for a while in silence and then he suddenly asked the other man point-blank whether if it came to blows with someone like Captain Scarfield he would make a fight of it.

The Quaker trading captain regarded him for a while in silence. His look, it seemed to Mainwaring, appeared to express doubt as to how far he dared to be frank. "Friend James," he said at last, "I may as well acknowledge that my officers and crew are somewhat worldly. They do not hold the same beliefs as I. I am inclined to think that if it came to the point of a fight with those evil men, my individual voice cast for peace would not be sufficient to keep my crew from meeting violence with violence. As for myself, thou knowest who I am and what my beliefs are in these matters."

Mainwaring made no comment as to the extremely questionable manner in which the Quaker proposed to beat the Devil at his own game. Then he asked his second question:

"And might I inquire," he said, "what you are doing here, and why you find it necessary to come at all into such a wicked, dangerous place as this?"

"Indeed, I knew thee would ask that question of me," said the Friend, "and I will be entirely frank with thee. These men of blood are, after all, only human beings, and as human beings they need food. I have at present upon this vessel more than 250 barrels of flour which will bring a higher price here than anywhere else in the West Indies. To be entirely frank with thee, I will tell thee that I was engaged in making a bargain for the sale of most of my merchandise when the news of thy approach drove away my best customer."

Mainwaring sat for a while in silence. What the captain had told him explained many things he had not understood before. It explained why Captain Cooper got almost as much for his flour and cornmeal now that peace had been declared as he had obtained when the war and the blockade were in full swing. It explained why he had been so strong a defender of Captain Scarfield and the pirates that afternoon in the garden. Meantime, what was to be done? Eleazer confessed openly that he dealt with the pirates. What now was his—Mainwaring's—duty in the case? Was the cargo of the *Eliza Cooper* contraband and subject to confiscation? And then another question framed itself in his mind: Who was this customer whom his approach had driven away?

As though Mainwaring had actually spoken his question, the captain began directly to speak about the subject. "I know," he said, "that in a moment thou will ask me who was this customer of whom I have just spoken. I have no desire to conceal his name from thee. It was the man known as Captain Jack or Captain John Scarfield."

Mainwaring almost jumped from his seat. "The Devil you say!" he cried. "And how long has it been," he asked, "since he left you?"

The Quaker skipper carefully refilled his pipe, which he had by now smoked out. "I would judge," he said, "that it is a matter of four or five hours since news was brought overland by means of swift runners of thy approach. Immediately the man of wickedness disappeared." Here Eleazer set the bowl of his pipe to the candle flame and began puffing out clouds of smoke. "I would have thee understand, James Mainwaring," he resumed, "that I am no friend of this wicked and sinful man. His safety is nothing to me. It is only a question of buying upon his part and of selling upon mine. If it is any satisfaction to thee I will heartily promise to bring thee news if I hear anything of the man of the Devil. I may furthermore say that I think it is likely thou will have news more or less directly of him within the space of a day. If this should happen, however, thou will have to do thy own fighting without help from me, for I am no man of combat nor of blood and will take no hand in it either way."

It struck Mainwaring that the words contained some meaning that did not appear upon the surface. When he went aboard the *Yankee* he confided his suspicions to his second in command, Lieutenant Underwood. As night descended he had a double watch set and had everything prepared to repel any attack or surprise that might be attempted.

III

Nighttime in the tropics descends with a surprising speed. At one moment the earth is shining with the brightness of the twilight; in the next moment all things are suddenly swallowed into a gulf of darkness. The particular night of this story was not entirely clear; the time of year was about the approach of the rainy season, and the tropical clouds added obscurity to the darkness of the sky, so that the night fell with even more startling quickness than usual. The blackness was very dense. Now and then a group of drifting stars swam out of a rift in the vapors, but the night was strangely silent and of a velvety darkness.

As the obscurity deepened, Mainwaring ordered lanterns to be lit and slung to the stays, and the faint yellow of their illumination lit the white of the snug little war vessel, gleaming here and there in a starlike spark upon the brass trimmings and causing the rows of cannons to assume gigantic proportions.

For some reason Mainwaring was possessed by a strange, uneasy feeling. He walked restlessly up and down the deck for a time, and then, still full of mysterious anxieties, went into his cabin to finish writing his log for the day. He unstrapped his cutlass and laid it upon the table, lit his pipe at the lantern, and was about to lay aside his coat when word was brought to him that the captain of the trading schooner had come alongside and had some private information to communicate to him.

Mainwaring guessed in an instant that the trader's visit related somehow to news of Captain Scarfield, and as immediately, in the relief of something positive to face, all of his feeling of restlessness vanished like a shadow of mist. He gave orders that Captain Cooper should be immediately shown into the cabin, and in a few moments the tall, angular form of the Quaker skipper appeared in the narrow, lantern-lighted space.

Mainwaring at once saw that his visitor was strangely agitated and disturbed. He had taken off his hat, and shining beads of perspiration had gathered and stood clustered upon his forehead. He did not reply to Mainwaring's greeting; he did not, indeed, seem to hear it; but he came directly forward to the table and stood leaning with one hand upon the open log book in which the lieutenant had just been writing. Mainwaring had reseated himself at

the head of the table, and the tall figure of the skipper stood looking down at him.

"James Mainwaring," he said, "I promised thee to report if I had
news of the pirate. Art thou ready now to hear my news?"

There was something so strange in his agitation that it began to
infect Mainwaring with a feeling somewhat similar to that which
appeared to disturb his visitor. "I do not know what you mean, sir,"
he cried, "by asking if I care to hear your news. At this moment I
would rather have news of that scoundrel than to have anything I
know of in the world."

"Thou would? Thou would?" cried the other, with mounting
agitation. "Art thou in such haste to meet him as all that? Very
well; very well, then. Suppose I could bring thee face to face with
him—what then? Hey? Hey? Face to face with him, James
Mainwaring!"

The thought instantly flashed into Mainwaring's mind that the
pirate had returned to the island—that perhaps at that moment he
was somewhere near.

"I do not understand you, sir," he cried. "Do you mean to tell
me that you know where the villain is? If so, lose no time in inform-
ing me, for every instant of delay may mean his chance of again
escaping."

"No danger of that!" the other declared, vehemently. "No danger of that! I'll tell thee where he is and I'll bring thee to him quick
enough!" And as he spoke he thumped his fist against the open log
book. In his growing excitement his eyes appeared to shine green in
the lantern light, and the sweat that had stood in beads upon his
forehead was now running in streams down his face; one drop hung
like a jewel from the tip of his beaklike nose. He came a step nearer
to Mainwaring and bent forward toward him, and there was something so strange and ominous in his bearing that the lieutenant
instinctively drew back a little where he sat.

"Captain Scarfield has sent something to you," said Eleazer, almost in a raucous voice, "something that you will be surprised to see." And the lapse in his speech from the Quaker "thee" to the more usual "you" struck Mainwaring as very strange.

As he was speaking, Eleazer was fumbling in a pocket of his long-tailed drab coat, and then he brought something forth that gleamed in the lantern light.

The next moment Mainwaring saw pointed directly in his face the round and hollow nozzle of a pistol.

There was an instant of dead silence, and then: "I am the man you seek!" said Eleazer Cooper, in a tense and breathless voice.

The whole thing had happened so instantaneously and unexpectedly that for the moment Mainwaring sat like one petrified. Had a thunderbolt fallen from the silent sky and burst at his feet he could not have been more stunned. He was like one trapped in a horrible nightmare, and he gazed as through a mist into the well-known, sober face now transformed, as from within, into the aspect of a devil. That face, now ashy white, was distorted into a diabolical grin. The teeth glistened in the lamplight. The brows, twisted into a tense and convulsed frown, were drawn down into black shadows, through which the eyes burned a glowing green like the eyes of a wild animal. Again he spoke in the same breathless voice. "I am John Scarfield! Look at me, then, if you want to see a pirate!" Again there was a short moment of silence, through which Mainwaring heard his watch ticking loudly from where it hung against the bulkhead. Then once more the other began speaking. "You would chase me out of the West Indies, would you? What have you come to now? You are caught in your own trap, and you'll squeal loud enough before you get out of it. Speak a word or make a movement and I'll blow your brains out against the partition behind you! Listen to what I say or you are a dead man. Sing out an order instantly for my mate and my bos'n to come here to the cabin, and be quick about it, for my finger's on the trigger, and it's only a pull to shut your mouth forever."

It was astonishing to Mainwaring, in afterward thinking about it all, how quickly his mind began to recover its steadiness after that first astonishing shock. Even as the pirate was speaking he discovered that his mind was clearing; his thoughts were becoming rearranged, and with a marvelous activity and an alertness he had never before experienced. He knew that if he moved to escape or uttered any outcry he instantly would be a dead man, for the circle of the pistol barrel was directed against his forehead with the steadiness of a rock. If he could for an instant divert that fixed and deadly attention he might still have a chance for life. With that thought, an inspiration burst into his mind and he instantly put it into execution; thought, inspiration, and action, as in a flash, were one. He must make the pirate turn aside his deadly gaze, and instantly he roared out in a voice that stunned his own ears: "Strike, bos'n! Strike, quick!"

Taken by surprise, and thinking, undoubtedly, that another enemy stood behind him, the pirate swung around like a flash with his pistol leveled against the blank boarding. But almost instantly he saw the trick that had been played upon him and in a second flash had turned again. The turn and return had occupied only a moment of time, but that moment had probably saved Mainwaring's life. As the pirate turned away his gaze for that brief instant Mainwaring leaped forward and upon him. There was a flashing flame of fire as the pistol was discharged and a deafening detonation that seemed to split his brain. For a moment, with reeling senses, he thought himself shot, but the next thing he knew he had escaped. With the energy of despair he swung his enemy around and drove him violently against the corner of the table. The pirate emitted a grunting cry and then they fell together, Mainwaring upon the top, and the pistol clattered with them to the floor in their fall. Even as he fell, Mainwaring roared in a voice of thunder, "All hands repel boarders!" And then again, "All hands repel boarders!"

Whether hurt by the table edge or not, the fallen pirate struggled as though possessed of forty devils, and in a moment or two Mainwaring saw the shine of a long, keen knife that he had drawn from somewhere under his clothes. The lieutenant caught him by the wrist, but the other's muscles were as though made of steel. They both fought in despairing silence, the one to carry out his frustrated purposes to kill, the other to save his life. Again and again Mainwaring felt that the knife had been thrust against him, piercing once his arm, once his shoulder, and again his neck. He felt the warm blood streaming down his arm and body and looked about him in despair. The pistol lay nearby, on the deck of the cabin. Still holding the pirate by the wrist, Mainwaring snatched up the empty weapon and struck once, then again, at the bald, narrow forehead beneath him. A third blow he delivered with all the force he could command, and then with a violent and convulsive gesture the straining muscles beneath him relaxed and grew limp, and the fight was won.

Through all the struggle he had been aware of the shouts of voices, of the trampling of feet and the discharge of firearms, and the thought came to him, even through his own danger, that the *Yankee* was being assaulted by the pirates. As he felt the struggling form beneath him loosen and dissolve into unconsciousness, he leaped up; snatching his cutlass, which still lay upon the table, he rushed out upon the deck, leaving the stricken form lying twitching upon the floor behind him.

It was a fortunate thing that he had set double watches and prepared himself for some attack from the pirates, otherwise the *Yankee* would certainly have been lost. As it was, the surprise was so overwhelming that the pirates, who had been concealed in the large whaleboat that had come alongside, were not only able to gain a foothold upon the deck, but for a time it seemed as though they would drive the crew of the brig below the hatches.

But as Mainwaring, streaming with blood, rushed out onto the deck, the pirates became immediately aware that their own captain must have been overpowered, and in an instant their desperate energy began to evaporate. One or two jumped overboard. One, who seemed to be the mate, fell dead from a pistol shot. And then there was a rush of a retreat and a vision of leaping forms in the dusky light of the lanterns and a sound of splashing in the water below.

The crew of the *Yankee* continued firing at the wakes of the swimming bodies, but whether with any effect it was impossible at the time to tell.

IV

The pirate captain did not die immediately. He lingered for three or four days, now and then unconscious, now and then semi-conscious, but always delirious. While he lay dying, the woman with whom he lived in this part of his extraordinary dual existence nursed and cared for him. In the wanderings of his mind the same duality of life followed him. Now and then he would appear the calm, sober, self-contained, well-ordered member of a peaceful society that his friends in his far-away home knew him to be; at other times the nether part of his nature would leap into life like a wild beast, furious and gnashing. At the one time he talked evenly and clearly of peaceful things; at the other time he blasphemed and hooted with fury.

Several times Mainwaring, though racked by his own wounds, sat beside the dying man through the silent watches of the tropical nights. Often upon these occasions as he looked at the thin, lean face babbling and talking so aimlessly, he wondered what it all meant. Could it have been madness—madness in which the separate entities of good and bad each had, in its turn, a perfect and distinct existence? He chose to think that this was the case. Who, within his inner consciousness, does not feel that same bestial, savage man struggling against the stern bonds of morality and civilized behavior? Were those bonds burst, as it was with this man, might not the wild beast rush forth, as it had rushed forth in him? Such were the questions that Mainwaring asked himself. And how had it all come about? By what easy steps had the respectable Quaker skipper descended from the calm and order of his home life into such a pit of iniquity? Many such thoughts passed through Mainwaring's mind, and he pondered them through the still tropical nights while he sat watching the pirate captain struggle out of the world he had so long burdened. At last the poor wretch died, and the earth was rid of one of its torments.

A systematic search was made through the island for the scattered crew, but none was captured. Either there were some secret hiding places upon the island (which was not very likely) or else they had escaped in boats hidden somewhere among the tropical foliage. At any rate they were gone.

Nor, search as he would, could Mainwaring find a trace of any of the pirate treasure. After the pirate's death and under close

questioning, Scarfield's woman broke down and confessed in broken English that Captain Scarfield had taken a quantity of silver money aboard his vessel, but either she was mistaken or else the pirates had taken it from there and had hidden it somewhere else.

Nor would the treasure ever have been found but for a most fortunate accident.

Mainwaring had given orders that the *Eliza Cooper* was to be burned, and a party was detailed to carry out the order. At this the cook of the *Yankee* came petitioning for some of the Wilmington and Brandywine flour to make some plum pudding, and Mainwaring granted his request; he ordered one of the men to knock open one of the barrels of flour and to supply the cook's demands.

The crew detailed to execute this modest order in connection with the destruction of the pirate vessel had not been gone a quarter of an hour when word came back that the hidden treasure had been found.

Mainwaring hurried aboard the *Eliza Cooper*, and there in the midst of the open flour barrel he beheld a great amount of silver coin buried in, and partly covered by, the white meal. A systematic search was now made. One by one the flour barrels were heaved up from below and burst open on the deck and their contents searched, and if nothing but the meal was found it was swept overboard. The breeze was whitened with clouds of flour, and the white meal covered the surface of the ocean for yards around.

In all, more than $150,000 was found concealed beneath the innocent flour and meal. It was no wonder the pirate captain was so successful, when he could upon an instant's notice transform himself from a wolf of the ocean to a peaceful Quaker trader selling flour to the hungry towns and settlements among the scattered islands of the West Indies, and then carry his bloody treasure safely into his quiet Northern home.

Finally, it may be added that a wide strip of canvas painted black was discovered in the hold of the *Eliza Cooper*. Upon it, in great white letters, was painted the name "The Bloodhound." Undoubtedly this was used upon occasions to cover the real and peaceful title of the trading schooner, just as its captain had, in reverse, covered his bloody and cruel life by a thin sheet of morality and respectability.

This is the true story of the death of Captain Jack Scarfield.

It is not likely that anyone ever identified Eleazer Cooper with the pirate, for only Mainwaring of all the crew of the *Yankee* was exactly aware of the true identity of Captain Scarfield. All that was ever known to the world was that Eleazer Cooper had been killed in a fight with the pirates.

In a little less than a year Mainwaring was married to Lucinda Fairbanks. As for Eleazer Cooper's fortune, which eventually came into the possession of Mainwaring through his wife, it was many times a subject of speculation to the lieutenant how it had been earned. There were times when he felt that a part of it at least was the fruit of piracy, but it was entirely impossible to guess how much more was the result of legitimate trading.

For a little time it seemed to Mainwaring that he should give it all up, but this idea was so impractical that he abandoned it, and in time his doubts faded away and he settled himself down to enjoy that which had come to him through his marriage.

In time the Mainwarings moved to New York, and ultimately the fortune that the pirate Scarfield had left behind him was used in part to found the great shipping house of Mainwaring & Bigot, whose famous transatlantic packet ships were in their time the admiration of the whole world.

Tom Chist
and the Treasure-Box

I

To tell about Tom Chist, and how he got his name, and how he came to be living at the little settlement of Henlopen just inside the mouth of Delaware Bay, the story must begin as far back as 1686, when a great storm swept the Atlantic coast from end to end. During the heaviest part of the hurricane a boat went ashore on the Hen-and-Chicken Shoals, just below Cape Henlopen and at the mouth of Delaware Bay, and Tom Chist was the only soul of all those on board the ill-fated vessel who escaped alive.

This story must first be told, since it was because of his strange and miraculous escape at that time that he gained the name given to him.

Even as late as that time of the American colonies, the little scattered settlement at Henlopen, made up of English, with a few Dutch and Swedish people, was still only a speck of life upon the vast frontier of the great American wilderness that spread with swamp and forest, no one knew how far to the west. That wilderness was not only full of wild beasts, but of Indians, who every autumn would come in wandering tribes, no one knew from where, to spend the winter along the shores of the freshwater lakes below Henlopen. There for four or five months they would live upon fish and clams and wild ducks and geese, chipping their arrowheads and making their earthenware pots and pans under the shelter of the sand-hills and pine woods below the capes.

Sometimes on Sundays, when the Reverend Hillary Jones would be preaching in the little log church back in the woods, these half-clad Indians would come in from the cold and sit squatting in the back of the church, listening to the words that had no meaning for them.

But about the wreck of the boat in 1686 . . . Such a wreck as that which then went ashore on the Hen-and-Chicken Shoals was a godsend to the poor and needy settlers in the wilderness where so few good things ever came. For the vessel went to pieces during the night, and the next morning the beach was strewn with wreckage—boxes and barrels, chests and poles, timbers and planks, a plentiful and bountiful harvest to be gathered up by the settlers as they chose, with no one to forbid or prevent them.

The name of the boat, as found painted on some of the water-barrels and sea-chests, was the *Bristol Merchant*, and she presumedly hailed from England.

And the only soul who escaped alive from the wreck was Tom Chist.

A settler, a fisherman named Matt Abrahamson, and his daughter Molly found Tom. He was washed up on the beach among the wreckage, in a great wooden box which had been securely tied around with a rope and lashed between two poles—apparently for better protection in beating through the surf. Matt Abrahamson thought he had found something of more than usual value when he came upon this chest. But when he cut the cords and broke open the box with his ax, he could not have been more astonished: he beheld a baby, nine or ten months old, lying half smothered in the blankets that covered the bottom of the box.

Matt Abrahamson's daughter Molly's own baby had died a month or so before. So when she saw the little one lying there in the bottom of the chest, she cried out in a loud voice that the Good Man had sent her another baby in place of her own.

The rain was driving before the hurricane storm in dim, slanting sheets, and so she wrapped up the baby in the man's coat she wore, and ran off home without waiting to gather up any more of the wreckage.

It was Parson Jones who gave the foundling his name. When the news came to his ears of what Matt Abrahamson had found, he went over to the fisherman's cabin to see the child. He examined the clothes in which the baby was dressed. They were of fine linen and handsomely stitched, and the reverend gentleman's opinion was that the foundling's parents must have been well off. A kerchief had been wrapped around the baby's neck and under its arms and tied behind, and in the corner, marked with very fine needlework, were the initials "T. C."

"What d'ye call him, Molly?" said Parson Jones. He was standing, as he spoke, with his back to the fire, warming his palms before the blaze. The pocket of the greatcoat he wore bulged out with a big bottle of spirits which he had taken from the wreck that afternoon. "What d'ye call him, Molly?"

"I'll call him Tom, after my own baby."

"That goes very well with the initial on the kerchief," said Parson Jones. "But what other name d'ye give him? Let it be something to go with the C."

"I don't know," said Molly.

"Why not call him Chist, since he was born in a chist out of the sea? 'Tom Chist'—the name goes off like a flash in the pan." And so Tom Chist he was called, and Tom Chist he was christened.

So much for the beginning of the history of Tom Chist. The story of Captain Kidd's treasure-box does not begin until the late spring of 1699.

That was the year that the famous pirate captain, coming up from the West Indies, sailed his sloop into Delaware Bay, where he lay for over a month waiting for news from his friends in New York.

For he had sent word to that town asking if the coast was clear for him to return home with the rich prize he had brought from the Indian seas and the coast of Africa, and meantime he lay there in Delaware Bay waiting for his reply. Before he left he turned the whole of Tom Chist's life topsy-turvy with something that he brought ashore.

By that time Tom Chist had grown into a strong-limbed, thick-jointed boy of fourteen or fifteen years of age. It was a miserable dog's life he lived with old Matt Abrahamson, for the old fisherman was drunk more than half the time, and when he was in that state there was hardly a day that passed when he did not give Tom a curse or even an actual beating. One would have thought that such treatment would have broken the spirit of the poor little foundling, but it had just the opposite effect upon Tom Chist, who was one of those stubborn, sturdy, stiff-willed fellows who only grow harder and more tough the more they are treated badly. It had been a long time now since he had made any outcry or complaint at the ill-treatment he suffered from old Matt. At such times he would shut his teeth and bear whatever came to him, until sometimes the boozy old Abrahamson would be driven almost mad by his stubborn silence. Maybe he would stop in the midst of some ill-treatment that he was administering, and, grinding his teeth, would cry out: "Won't ye say anything? Won't ye say anything? Well, then, I'll see if I can't make ye say something!" When things had reached such a state as this, Molly would generally interfere to protect her foster son, and then she and Tom would fight the old man together until they had wrenched the stick or the strap out of his hand. Then old Matt would chase them out of doors and around and around the house for maybe half an hour until his anger was cool, and for a time the storm would be over.

Besides his foster mother, Tom Chist had a very good friend in Parson Jones, who used to come over every now and then to Abrahamson's hut hoping to get a half-dozen fish for breakfast. He always had a kind word or two for Tom, who during the winter evenings would go over to the good man's house to learn his letters, and to read and write and cipher a little, so that by now he was able to spell the words out of the Bible and the almanac and even knew some arithmetic.

This is the sort of boy Tom Chist was, and this is the sort of the life he led. In the late spring or early summer of 1699, Captain Kidd's sloop sailed into the mouth of Delaware Bay and changed the whole fortune of his life.

And this is the story of Captain Kidd's treasure-box.

II

Old Matt Abrahamson kept the flat-bottomed boat in which he went out fishing some distance down the shore, and in the neighborhood of the old wreck that had been sunk on the shoals. This was the usual fishing-ground of the settlers, and here old Matt's boat generally lay drawn up on the sand.

There had been a thunderstorm that afternoon, and Tom had gone down the beach to bale out the boat against the morning's fishing. It was an evening full of moonlight now, as he was returning, and the night sky was filled with floating clouds. Now and then there was a dull flash to the west, and once a muttering growl of thunder, promising another storm to come.

All that day the pirate sloop had been lying just off the shore at the back of the capes, and now Tom Chist could see the sails glimmering in the moonlight, spread for drying after the storm. He was walking up the shore homeward when he became aware that at some distance ahead of him there was a boat drawn up on the little narrow beach; a group of men were clustered around it. He hurried forward with a good deal of curiosity to see who had landed, but it was not until he had come close to them that he could distinguish who and what they were. Then he knew that it must be a party that had come from the pirate sloop. They had evidently just landed, and two men were lifting out a chest from the boat. One of them was a black man, naked to the waist, and the other was a white man in his shirt sleeves, wearing petticoat breeches, a Monteray cap on his head, a red bandanna kerchief around his neck, and gold earrings in his ears. He had a long braid of hair hanging down his back and a great sheath-knife dangling from his side. Another man, evidently the captain of the party, stood a little distance away as they lifted the chest out of the boat. He had a cane in one hand and a lit lantern in the other, although the moon was shining as bright as day. He wore jack-boots and a handsome laced coat, and he had a long drooping mustache that curled down below his chin. He wore a fine feathered hat, and his long black hair hung down upon his shoulders.

They were so busy lifting the chest from the boat that at first they did not observe that Tom Chist had come up and was standing there. It was the man with the long braid and the gold earrings that spoke to him. "Boy, what do you want here, boy?" he said, in a rough, hoarse voice. "Where d'ye come from?" And then dropping his end of the chest, and without giving Tom time to answer, he pointed off down the beach, and said, "You'd better be going about your own business, if you know what's good for you. And don't you come back, or you'll find what you don't want waiting for you."

Tom saw in a glance that the pirates were all looking at him, and then, without saying a word, he turned and walked away. The man who had spoken to him followed him threateningly for a short distance, as though to see that he had gone away as he was told to do. But soon he stopped, and Tom hurried on alone, until the boat and the crew and all were lost in the moonlit night. Then he himself stopped also, turned, and looked back toward where he had left.

There had been something very strange in the appearance of the men he had just seen, something very mysterious in their actions, and he wondered what it all meant, and what they were going to do. He stood for a little while looking and listening. He could see nothing, and could hear only the sound of distant talking. What were they doing on the lonely shore at night? Then, following a sudden impulse, he turned and cut off across the sand humps, skirting around inland, but keeping pretty close to the shore; his object was to spy upon them and to watch what they were doing from the back of the sand-hills that fronted the beach.

He had gone along some distance when he became aware of the sound of voices that seemed to be drawing closer to him as he came toward the speakers. He stopped and stood listening, and instantly, as he stopped, the voices stopped also. He crouched there silently in the bright, glimmering moonlight, surrounded by the silent stretches of sand, and the stillness seemed to press upon him like a heavy hand. Then suddenly the sound of a man's voice began again, and as Tom listened he could hear someone slowly counting. "Ninety-one," the voice began, "ninety-two, ninety-three, ninety-four, ninety-five, ninety-six, ninety-seven, ninety-eight, ninety-nine, one hundred, one hundred and one"—the slow, monotonous count coming nearer and nearer to him—"one hundred and two, one hundred and three, one hundred and four," and so on.

Suddenly he saw three heads appear above the sand-hill, so close to him that he crouched down quickly with a keen thrill, beside the mound near which he stood. His first fear was that they might have seen him in the moonlight; but they had not, and his heart rose again as the counting voice went steadily on. "One hundred and twenty," it was saying—"and twenty-one, and twenty-two, and twenty-three, and twenty-four," and then he who was counting came out from behind the little sandy rise into the white and open level of shimmering brightness.

It was the man with the cane whom Tom had seen some time before—the captain of the party that had landed. He carried his cane under his arm now, and was holding his lantern close to something that he held in his hand, and upon which he looked narrowly as he walked with a slow and measured tread in a perfectly straight line across the sand, counting each step as he took it. "And twenty-five, and twenty-six, and twenty-seven, and twenty-eight, and twenty-nine, and thirty."

Behind him walked two other figures, the ones whom Tom had seen lifting the chest out of the boat. Now they were carrying the heavy box between them, laboring through the sand with shuffling steps as they bore it onward.

As he who was counting pronounced the word "thirty," the two men set the chest down on the sand with a grunt, the man with the earrings panting and blowing and wiping his sleeve across his forehead. And immediately he who counted took out a slip of paper and marked something down upon it. They stood there for a long time, during which Tom lay behind the sand-hill watching them, and for a while the silence was uninterrupted. In the perfect stillness Tom could hear the washing of the little waves beating upon the distant beach, and once the faraway sound of a laugh from one of those who stood by the boat.

One, two, three minutes passed, and then the men picked up the chest and started on again; and then again the other man began his counting. "Thirty and one, and thirty and two, and thirty and three, and thirty and four"—he walked straight across the level open, still looking intently at that which he held in his hand—"and thirty and five, and thirty and six, and thirty and seven," and so on, until the three figures disappeared in the little hollow between the two sand-hills on the opposite side of the open, and still Tom could hear the sound of the counting voice in the distance.

Just as they disappeared behind the hill there was a sudden faint flash of light; and as Tom lay still listening to the counting, he heard, after a long interval, a faraway muffled rumble of distant thunder. He waited for a while, and then arose and stepped to the top of the sand-hill behind which he had been lying. He looked all about him, but there was no one else to be seen. Then he stepped down from the mound and followed in the direction in which the pirate captain and the two men carrying the chest had gone. He crept along cautiously, stopping now and then to make sure that he still heard the counting voice, and when it ceased he laid down upon the sand and waited until it began again.

So following the pirates, he saw the three figures again in the distance, and, skirting around the back of a hill of sand covered with coarse grass, he came to where he overlooked a little open, level space gleaming white in the moonlight.

The three had been crossing the level of sand and were now not more than twenty-five paces from him. They had again set down the chest, upon which the white man with the long braid and the gold earrings had seated to rest himself, the black man standing close beside him. The moon shone as bright as day and fully upon his face. It was looking directly at Tom Chist, every line as keenly cut with white lights and black shadows as though it had been carved in ivory and ebony. He sat perfectly motionless, and Tom drew back, startled, almost thinking he had been discovered. He lay silent, his heart beating heavily in his throat; but there was no alarm, and soon he heard the counting begin again, and when he looked once more, he saw they were going away, straight across the little open. A soft, sliding hill of sand lay directly in front of them. They did not turn aside but went straight over it, the leader helping himself up the sandy slope with his cane, still counting, and still keeping his eyes fixed upon that which he held in his hand. Then they disappeared again behind the white crest on the other side.

So Tom followed them cautiously until they had gone almost half a mile inland. When he saw them clearly again, it was from a little grassy rise which looked down like the crest of a bowl upon the floor of sand below. Upon this smooth white floor the moon beat with almost dazzling brightness.

The white man who had helped to carry the chest was now kneeling, busy at some work, though what it was Tom at first could not see. He was whittling the point of a stick into a long wooden peg, and when he had finished what he was doing, he arose and stepped to where he who seemed to be the captain had stuck his cane upright into the ground, as though to mark some particular spot. He drew the cane out of the sand, thrusting the stick down in its stead. Then he drove the long peg down with a wooden mallet which the black man handed to him. The sharp rapping of the mallet upon the top of the peg sounded loud in the perfect stillness, and Tom lay watching and wondering what it all meant. The man, with quick repeated blows, drove the peg further and further down into the sand until it showed only two or three inches above the surface. As he finished his work there was another faint flash of light, and then another smothered rumble of thunder; Tom, as he looked out toward the west, saw the silver rim of the round and sharply outlined thundercloud rising slowly up into the sky and pushing the other broken, drifting clouds before it.

The two white men were now stooping over the peg, the black man watching them. Then the man with the cane began walking straight away from the peg, carrying the end of a measuring-line with him, the other end of which the man with the earrings held against the top of the peg. When the pirate captain had reached the end of the measuring-line he marked a cross upon the sand, and then again they measured out another stretch of space.

So they measured a distance five times over, and then, from where Tom lay, he could see the man with the braid drive another peg just at the foot of a sloping rise of sand that beyond swept up into a tall white dune that appeared sharp and clear against the night sky. As soon as the man with the braid had driven the second peg into the ground they began measuring again. And so, still measuring, they disappeared in another direction which took them in behind the sand dune, where Tom no longer could see what they were doing.

The black man still sat by the chest where the two had left him, only now he was looking all around him, and so bright and strong was the moonlight that from where he lay Tom could see the glint of it twinkling in his eyes.

Then from behind the hill there came, for the third time, the sharp rapping sound of the mallet driving still another peg, and after a while the two pirates emerged from behind the sloping whiteness into the space of moonlight again.

They came directly to where the chest lay. The white man and the black man lifting it once more, they walked across the level of open sand, and then on behind the edge of the hill and out of Tom's sight.

III

Tom Chist could no longer see what the pirates were doing; neither did he dare to cross over the open space of sand that now lay between them and him. He lay there speculating as to what was going on, and meantime the storm-cloud was rising higher and higher above the horizon, with louder and louder mutterings of thunder following each dull flash from out of the cavernous cloudy depths. In the silence he could hear an occasional click, as of some iron implement, and he thought that the pirates were burying the chest, though just where they were at work he could neither see nor tell.

Still he lay there watching and listening, and soon a puff of warm air blew across the sand, and a thumping tumble of louder thunder leaped from out the belly of the storm-cloud, which every minute was coming nearer and nearer. Still Tom Chist lay watching.

Suddenly, almost unexpectedly to him, the three figures reappeared from behind the sand-hill, the pirate captain leading the way, his two associates following closely behind him. They had gone just about halfway across the sandy level between the hill and the mound behind which Tom Chist lay, when the pirate with the earrings stopped and bent over as though to tie his shoe. This brought the black man a few steps in front of his companion.

That which then followed happened so suddenly, so unexpectedly, so swiftly, that Tom Chist had hardly time to realize what it all meant before it was over. As the black pirate passed him the other man arose suddenly and silently erect, and Tom Chist saw the white moonlight glint upon the blade of a long knife which he now held in his hand. He took one, two silent, catlike steps, and then there was a sweeping flash of the blade in the moonlight, and a blow, the thump of which Tom could distinctly hear even from where he lay stretched out upon the sand. There was an instant echoing yell from the stricken man, who ran stumbling forward, stopped, regained his footing, and then stood for an instant as though rooted to the spot.

Tom had distinctly seen the knife enter his back, and even thought that he had seen the glint of the point as it came out from the chest. Meantime the pirate captain had stopped, and now stood with his hand resting upon his cane looking calmly on.

The pirate with the braid stood for a while staring at the wounded man, who was now some distance away, and who was not very far from Tom when he staggered and fell. He tried to rise, then fell forward again, and then lay still. At that instant the first edge of the cloud cut across the moon, and there was a sudden darkness; but in the silence Tom heard the sound of another blow and a groan, and then a voice calling to the pirate captain that it was all over.

He saw the dim form of the captain crossing the level sand, and then, as the moon sailed out from behind the cloud, he saw one man standing over a figure that lay motionless upon the sand.

Then Tom Chist scrambled up and ran away, plunging down into the hollow of sand that lay in the shadows below. Over the next rise he ran, and down again into the next black hollow, and so on over the sliding, shifting ground, panting and gasping. It seemed

to him that he could hear footsteps following, and in the dreadful terror that possessed him he almost expected at any moment to feel the cold knife-blade slide between his own ribs in such a thrust from behind as he had seen given to the poor victim.

How he ran the distance he never could tell, but it was almost as in a dream that he found himself at last in front of old Matt Abrahamson's cabin, gasping, panting, and sobbing for breath, his feet dragging behind him like lumps of lead.

As he opened the door and dashed into the cabin there was a flash of light, and as he slammed to the door behind him there was an instant peal of thunder as though a great weight had been dropped upon the roof of the sky, so that the doors and windows of the cabin rattled.

IV

For Tom Chist it was a dreadful night of waking dreams mingled with the flashing lightning and the thunder of the storm that broke over the cottage, a downpour and beating of the rain upon the roof that lasted almost until morning.

Then came the dawning of a broad, wet daylight of sunshine that brought no relief.

As soon as he was up he went out of doors into the young day wet with the night's rain and gazed out toward the place where the mysterious sloop had been lying the day before.

It was no longer there.

It was some comfort to Tom to know that it was gone, and that it had taken those dreadful men with it. Were it not so he could not have walked a step through the day without a horrible fear that he might meet that horrible man with the long shining knife. He shuddered and gasped as a sudden keen memory of it all came upon him.

If he could only tell it to someone, he felt that it would be easier for him to bear. But then there was no one to whom he dared tell it; he could not tell it even to his foster mother.

There was something especially troubling for him in having to go out fishing with old Abrahamson that day, and it seemed to him that he suffered far more in the narrow, confined space of the little boat than he would have done upon the wide land, where he could walk about. His thoughts did not stop for an instant. Even when he was hauling in his wet and dripping line with a struggling fish at the end of it a memory of what he had seen would suddenly come upon him, and he would writhe and twist in spirit at the recollection. If he could only talk about it, even to old Abrahamson, it would be some relief. But when he looked at the old man's leathery face, at his lantern jaws cavernously chewing at a tobacco leaf, he felt that it was not possible for him to confide his terrible secret to him.

When the boat touched the shore again he leaped scrambling to the beach, with a feeling of great relief.

As soon as his dinner was eaten he ran away to find Parson Jones, and to pour out his troubles to those friendly ears.

He ran on, all the way from the hut to the parson's house, hardly stopping once in all the way, and when he knocked at the door he was panting and sobbing for breath.

The good man was sitting on the back-kitchen doorstep smoking his long pipe in the sunlight, while his wife within was rattling around among the pans and dishes in preparation of their supper, of which a strong porky smell already filled the air.

Tom Chist never could tell how he got his story told, but somehow, in convulsive fits and starts, panting and gasping for breath, he did manage to tell it all.

Parson Jones listened with breathless and perfect silence, broken only now and then by inarticulate sounds.

"And I don't know why they should have killed the poor black man," said Tom, as he finished his narrative.

"Why, that is very easy enough to understand," said the good reverend. " 'Twas a treasure-box they buried, Tom. A treasure-box! A treasure-box!"

In his excitement Mr. Jones had got up from his seat and was stamping up and down, puffing out great clouds of tobacco smoke into the hot air.

"A treasure-box?" cried out Tom.

"Ay, a treasure-box! And that was why they killed the poor black man. He was the only one, d'ye see, besides they two who knew the place where 'twas hid, and now that they've killed him out of the way, there's nobody but themselves knows. The villains— Tut, tut, look at that, now!" In his excitement the parson had snapped the stem of his pipe in two.

"Why, then," said Tom, "if that is so, 'tis indeed a wicked, bloody treasure, and fit to bring a curse upon anybody who finds it!"

" 'Tis more likely to bring a curse upon the soul who buried it," said Parson Jones. "And it may be a blessing to him who finds it. But tell me, Tom, do you think you could find the place again where 'twas hid?"

"I can't tell that," said Tom. " 'Twas all among the sand-hills, d'ye see, and it was at night as well. Maybe we could find the marks of their feet in the sand," he added.

" 'Tis not likely," said the reverend gentleman, "for the storm last night would have washed all that away."

"I could find the place," said Tom, "where the boat was drawn up on the beach."

"Why, then, that's something to start from, Tom," said his friend. "If we can find that, then maybe we can find where they went from there."

"If I was certain it was a treasure-box," cried out Tom Chist, "I would rake over every foot of sand between here and Henlopen to find it."

" 'Twould be like hunting for a needle in a haystack," said the Reverend Hillary Jones.

As Tom walked home, it seemed not only as though a ton's weight of gloom had been rolled away from his soul, but as though he could hardly contain himself with the prospect of treasure-hunting to look forward to.

V

The next day, early in the afternoon, Parson Jones and Tom Chist started off together, Tom carrying a spade over his shoulder, and the reverend gentleman walking along with his cane. As they jogged up the beach they talked together about the only thing they could talk about—the treasure-box. "And how big did you say 'twas?" asked the good gentleman.

"About so long," said Tom Chist, measuring off upon the spade, "and about so wide and this deep."

"And what if it should be full of money, Tom?" said the reverend gentleman, swinging his cane around and around in wide circles in the excitement of the thought, as he strode along briskly. "Suppose it should be full of money, what then?"

"By Moses!" said Tom Chist, hurrying to keep up with his friend. "I'd buy a ship for myself, I would, and I'd trade with India and with China, I would. Suppose the chist was all full of money, sir, and suppose we should find it—would there be enough in it, d'ye suppose, to buy a ship?"

"To be sure there would be enough, Tom; enough and to spare, and a good big lump over."

"And if I find it 'tis mine to keep, is it, and no mistake?"

"Why, to be sure it would be yours!" cried out the parson, in a loud voice. "To be sure it would be yours!" He knew nothing of the laws, but the doubt of the question began at once to ferment in his brain, and he strode along in silence for a while. "Whose else would it be but yours if you find it?" he burst out. "Can you tell me that?"

"If ever I have a ship of my own," said Tom Chist, "and if ever I sail to India in her, I'll fetch ye back the best chist of tea, sir, that ever was fetched from China."

Parson Jones burst out laughing. "Thankee, Tom," he said, "and I'll thankee again when I get my chist of tea. But tell me, Tom, didst thou ever hear of the farmer girl who counted her chickens before they were hatched?"

It was thus they talked as they hurried along up the beach together, and so came to a place at last where Tom stopped short and stood looking about him. " 'Twas just here," he said, "I saw the boat last night. Ay, I know 'twas here, for I remember that bit of wreck yonder, and that there was a tall stake drove in the sand just where that stake stands."

Parson Jones put on his spectacles and went over to the stake toward which Tom pointed. As soon as he had looked at it carefully, he called out: "Why, Tom, this hath just been driven down into the sand. 'Tis a brand-new stake of wood, and the pirates must have set it here themselves as a mark, just as they drove the pegs you spoke about down into the sand."

Tom came over and looked at the stake. It was a stout piece of oak nearly two inches thick; it had been shaped with some care, and the top of it had been painted red. He shook the stake and tried to move it, but it had been driven or planted so deeply into the sand that he could not stir it.

"Ay, sir," he said, "it must have been set here for a mark, for I'm sure 'twas not here yesterday or the day before." He stood looking all around him to see if there were other signs of the pirates' presence. At some distance away there was the corner of something white sticking up out of the sand. He could see that it was a scrap of paper, and he pointed to it, calling out,

"There's a piece of paper over there, sir. I wonder if they left that behind?"

If he had only known the miraculous chance that placed that paper there, he would not have walked over to it as carelessly as he did to pluck it up out of the sand. There was only an inch of it showing, and if it had not been for his sharp eyes, it would certainly have been overlooked and passed by. The next windstorm would have covered it up, and all that afterward happened never would have happened. "Look, sir," he said, as he struck the sand from it, "it has writing on it."

"Let me see it," said Parson Jones. He adjusted the spectacles a little more firmly on his nose as he took the paper in his hand and began reading it. "What's all this?" he said. "A whole lot of figures and nothing else." And then he read aloud. " 'Mark—S–SW by S' What d'ye suppose that means, Tom?"

"I don't know, sir," said Tom. "But maybe we can understand it better if we read on."

" 'Tis all a great lot of figures," said Parson Jones, "without a grain of meaning in them so far as I can see, unless they be sailing directions." And then he began reading again: " 'Mark—S–SW by S 40, 72, 91, 130, 151, 177, 202, 232, 256, 271'—d'ye see, it must be sailing directions—'299, 335, 362, 386, 415, 446, 469, 491, 522, 544, 571, 598'—what a lot of them there be—'626, 652, 676, 695, 724, 851, 876, 905, 940, 967. Peg. SE by E 269 foot. Peg. S–SW by S 427 foot. Peg. Dig to the west of this six foot.' "

"What's that about a peg?" exclaimed Tom. "What's that about a peg? And then there's something about digging too!" It was as though a sudden light began shining into his brain. He felt himself growing quickly very excited. "Read that over again, sir," he cried. "Why, sir, you remember I told you they drove a peg into the sand. And don't they say to dig close to it? Read it over again, sir—read it over again!"

"Peg?" said the good gentleman. "To be sure it was about a peg. Let's look again. Yes, here it is. 'Peg. SE by E 269 foot.' "

"Ay!" cried out Tom Chist again, in great excitement. "Don't you remember what I told you, sir, 269 foot? Surely that must be what I saw 'em measuring with the line."

Parson Jones had now caught the flame of excitement that began to blaze up so strongly in Tom's breast. He felt as though some wonderful thing was about to happen to them. "To be sure, to be sure!" he called out in a great big voice. "And then they measured out 427 foot west by south, and then they drove another peg, and then they buried the box six foot to the west of it. Why, Tom—why, Tom Chist! If we've read this right, thy fortune is made."

Tom Chist stood staring straight at the old gentleman's excited face, seeing nothing but it in all the bright infinity of sunshine. Were they indeed about to find the treasure-chest? He felt the sun very hot upon his shoulders, and he heard the harsh, insistent jarring of a tern that hovered and circled with forked tail and sharp white wings in the sunlight just above their heads. But all the time he stood staring into the good old gentleman's face.

It was Parson Jones who first spoke. "But what do all these figures mean?" And Tom observed how the paper shook and rustled in the tremor of excitement that shook his hand. He raised the paper to the focus of his spectacles and began to read again. " 'Mark. 40, 72, 91—' "

"Mark?" cried out Tom, almost screaming. "Why, that must mean the stake yonder; that must be the mark." And he pointed to the oak stick with its red tip blazing against the white shimmer of sand behind it.

"And the 40 and 72 and 91," cried the old gentleman, in a voice equally shrill—"why, that must mean the number of steps the pirate was counting when you heard him."

"To be sure, that's what they mean!" cried Tom Chist. "That is it, and it can be nothing else. Oh, come, sir—come, sir; let us make haste and find it!"

"Wait, wait!" said the good gentleman, holding up his hand; and again Tom Chist noticed how it trembled and shook. His voice was steady enough, though very hoarse, but his hand shook and trembled. "Wait! First of all, we must follow these measurements. And 'tis a marvelous thing," he croaked, after a little pause, "how this paper ever came to be here."

"Maybe it was blown here by the storm," suggested Tom Chist.

"Likely enough, likely enough," said Parson Jones. "Likely enough, after the wretches had buried the chest and killed that poor man, they were so buffeted about by the storm that it was shaken out of the man's pocket, and thus blew away from him without his knowing it."

"But let us find the box!" cried out Tom Chist, squirming in his excitement.

"Ay, ay," said the good man, "only wait a moment, my boy, until we make sure what we're doing. I've got my pocket-compass here, but we must have something to measure off the feet when we have found the peg. You run across to Tom Brooke's house and fetch that measuring-rod he used to lay out his new barn. While you're gone I'll pace off the distance marked on the paper with my pocket-compass."

VI

Tom Chist was gone for almost an hour, though he ran nearly all the way there and back, borne on the wings of his excitement. When he returned, panting, Parson Jones was nowhere to be seen, but Tom saw his footsteps leading away inland, and he followed the scuffling marks in the smooth surface across the sand humps and down into the hollows, and soon he found the good gentleman in a spot he at once knew as soon as he laid his eyes upon it.

It was the open space where the pirates had driven their first peg, and where Tom Chist had afterward seen them kill the poor black man. Tom Chist gazed around as though expecting to see some sign of the tragedy, but the space was as smooth and as undisturbed as a floor, except where, midway across it, Parson Jones, who was now stooping over something on the ground, had trampled on it.

When Tom Chist saw him, he was still bending over, scraping the sand away from something he had found.

It was the first peg!

Within half an hour they had found the second and third pegs, and Tom Chist stripped off his coat and began digging like mad down into the sand, Parson Jones standing over him and watching. The sun was sloping more than halfway toward the west when the blade of Tom Chist's spade struck something hard.

If it had been his own heart that he had hit in the sand his breast could hardly have more thrilled.

It was the treasure-box!

Parson Jones himself leaped down into the hole and began scraping away the sand with his hands as though he had gone crazy. At last, with some difficulty, they tugged and hauled the chest up out of the sand to the surface, where it lay covered all over with the grit that clung to it.

It was securely locked and fastened with a padlock, and it took a good many blows with the blade of the spade to burst the bolt. Parson Jones himself lifted the lid.

Tom Chist leaned forward and gazed down into the open box. He would not have been surprised to have seen it filled full of yellow gold and bright jewels. It was half full of books and papers, and half full of canvas bags tied safely and securely with cords of string.

Parson Jones lifted out one of the bags, and it jingled as he did so. It was full of money.

He cut the string, and with trembling, shaking hands, handed the bag to Tom, who, in an ecstasy of wonder and dizzy delight, poured out with swimming sight upon the coat spread on the

ground a mass of shining silver money that rang and twinkled and jingled as it fell in a shining heap upon the coarse cloth.

Parson Jones raised both hands into the air, and Tom stared at what he saw, wondering whether it was all so, and whether he was really awake. It seemed to him as though he was in a dream.

There were twenty-two bags in all in the chest; ten of them full of silver money, eight of them full of gold money, three of them full of gold dust, and one small bag with jewels wrapped up in cotton and paper.

" 'Tis enough," cried out Parson Jones, "to make us both rich men as long as we live."

The burning summer sun, though sloping in the sky, beat down upon them as hot as fire; but neither of them noticed it. Neither did they notice hunger nor thirst nor fatigue, but sat there as though in a trance, with the bags of money piled up on the sand all around them, a great pile of money heaped upon the coat, and the open chest beside them. It was almost sundown by the time Parson Jones had begun to examine the books and papers in the chest.

Of the three books, two were evidently log-books of the pirates who had been lying off the mouth of Delaware Bay all this time. The other book was written in Spanish and was evidently the log-book of some captured prize.

It was then, sitting there upon the sand, the good old gentleman reading in his high cracking voice, that they first learned from the bloody records in those two books who it was who had been sailing about the cape all this time, and that it was the famous Captain Kidd. Every now and then the reverend gentleman would stop to exclaim, "Oh, the bloody wretch!" or, "Oh, the desperate, cruel villains!" and then would go on reading again a scrap here and a scrap there.

And all the while Tom Chist sat and listened, every now and

then reaching out and touching the heap of money still lying upon the coat.

One might be inclined to wonder why Captain Kidd had kept those bloody records. He had probably laid them away because they so incriminated many of the great people of the colony of New York that, with the books in evidence, it would have been impossible to bring the pirate to justice without dragging a dozen or more fine rich gentlemen down with him. If he could have kept them in his own possession, they would doubtless have been a great weapon of defense to protect him from the gallows. Indeed, when Captain Kidd was finally brought to conviction and hung, he was not accused of his piracies, but of striking a mutinous seaman upon the head with a bucket and accidentally killing him. They did not dare to accuse him of his piracies. He was really hung because he was a pirate, and we know that it was the log-books that Tom Chist brought to New York that did the trick. But what he was accused and convicted of was the killing of his own ship-carpenter with a bucket.

So Parson Jones, as he and Tom Chist sat there in the slanting light, skimmed through these terrible records of piracy, and Tom, with the pile of gold and silver money beside him, sat and listened to him.

What a spectacle, if anyone had come upon them! But they were alone, with only the vast arch of sky above them and the wide white stretch of sand around them. The sun sank lower and lower, until it slanted so far in the sky that there was only time to glance through the other papers in the chest.

They were nearly all goldsmiths' bills of exchange drawn in favor of some of the more prominent merchants of New York. Parson Jones, as he read over the names, knew of nearly all the gentlemen by hearsay. Ay, here was this gentleman; he thought that name would be among 'em. What? Here is Mr. So-and-so. Well, if all they say is true, the villain has robbed one of his own best friends.

"I wonder," he said, "why the wretch should have hidden these papers so carefully away with the other treasures, for they could do him no good." Then, answering his own question: "Likely because these will give him a hold over the gentlemen to whom they are drawn so that he can make a good bargain for his own neck before he gives the bills back to their owners. I'll tell you what you must do, Tom," he continued. "It is you yourself who shall go to New York and bargain for the return of these papers. 'Twill be as good as another fortune to you."

The majority of the bills were drawn in favor of one Richard Chillingsworth, Esq. "And he is," said Parson Jones, "one of the richest men in the province of New York. You shall go to him with the news of what we have found."

"When shall I go?" said Tom Chist.

"You shall go upon the very first boat we can catch," said the parson. He had turned, still holding the bills in his hand, and was now fingering over the pile of money that still lay tumbled out upon the coat. "I wonder, Tom," he said, "if you could spare me twenty or so of these coins?"

"You shall have a thousand, if you choose," said Tom, bursting with gratitude and with generosity in his newly found treasure.

"You are as fine a lad as ever I saw, Tom," said the parson, "and I'll thank you to the last day of my life."

Tom scooped up a double handful of silver money. "Take it, sir," he said, "and you may have as much more as you want of it."

He poured it into the dish that the good man made of his hands, and the parson made a motion as though to empty it into his pocket. Then he stopped, as though a sudden doubt had occurred to him. "I don't know that 'tis fit for me to take this pirate money, after all," he said.

"But you are welcome to it," said Tom.

Still the parson hesitated. "Nay," he burst out, "I'll not take it;

'tis blood-money." And as he spoke he chucked the whole double handful into the now empty chest, then arose and dusted the sand from his breeches. Then, with a great deal of bustling energy, he helped to tie the bags again and put them all back into the chest.

They reburied the chest in the place from where they had taken it, and then the parson folded the precious paper of directions, placed it carefully in his wallet, and his wallet in his pocket. "Tom," he said, for the twentieth time, "your fortune has been made this day."

And Tom Chist, as he rattled in his breeches pocket the half-dozen gold coins he had kept out of his treasure, felt that what his friend had said was true.

As the two went back homeward across the level space of sand, Tom Chist suddenly stopped and stood looking about him. " 'Twas just here," he said, digging his heel down into the sand, "that they killed the unfortunate black man."

"And here he lies buried for all time," said Parson Jones; and as he spoke he dug his cane down into the sand. Tom Chist shuddered. He would not have been surprised if the tip of the cane had struck something soft beneath that level surface. But it did not do so, nor was any sign of that tragedy ever seen again. For, whether the pirates had carried away what they had done and buried it elsewhere, or whether the storm in blowing the sand had completely leveled off and hidden all sign of that tragedy where it was enacted, it is certain that it never came to sight again—at least as far as Tom Chist and the Reverend Hillary Jones ever knew.

VII

This is the story of the treasure-box. All that remains now is to wind up the story of Tom Chist, and to tell of what came of him in the end.

He did not go back again to live with old Matt Abrahamson. Parson Jones had now taken charge of him and his fortunes, and Tom did not have to go back to the fisherman's hut.

Old Abrahamson talked a great deal about it, and would come to yell at good Parson Jones, threatening what he would do to Tom if he ever caught him for running away. But Tom on all these occasions kept carefully out of his way, and nothing came of the old man's threats.

Tom used to go over to see his foster mother now and then, but always when the old man was from home. And Molly Abrahamson used to warn him to keep out of her father's way. "He's in as vile a humor as ever I've seen, Tom," she said. "He sits sulking all day long, and 'tis my belief he'd kill ye if he caught ye."

Of course Tom said nothing, even to her, about the treasure, and he and the reverend gentleman kept it all to themselves. About three weeks later Parson Jones managed to get Tom shipped aboard a vessel bound for New York town, and a few days later Tom Chist landed at that place. He had never been in such a town before, and he marveled at the number of brick houses, at the multitude of people coming and going along the fine, hard earthen sidewalk, at the shops and the stores where goods hung in the windows, and, most of all, at the fortifications and the battery at the point, at the rows of threatening cannon, and at the scarlet-coated sentries pacing up and down the ramparts. All this was very wonderful, and so were the boats clustered at anchor in the harbor. It was like a new world, so different was it from the sand-hills and the grassy levels of Henlopen.

Tom Chist took up his lodgings at a coffeehouse close to the town wall, and from there he sent by the post-boy a letter written by Parson Jones to Mr. Chillingsworth. In a little while the boy returned with a message, asking Tom to come up to Chillingsworth's house that afternoon at two o'clock.

Tom accompanied the post-boy with a great deal of anxiety, and his heart fell away altogether when he found himself brought to a grand brick house, three stories high, with wrought-iron letters across the front.

The counting-house was in the same building; but Tom, because of Mr. Jones's letter, was conducted directly into the parlor, where the great rich man was awaiting his coming. He was sitting in a double-nailed armchair, smoking a pipe of tobacco, and with a bottle of fine old Madeira close to his elbow.

Tom had not yet had a chance to buy a new suit of clothes, so he made no special impression in the rough dress he had brought with him from Henlopen. Nor did Mr. Chillingsworth seem to think very highly of his appearance, but sat looking sideways at him as he smoked.

"Well, my lad," he said, "and what is this thing you have to tell me that is so wonderful? I got what's-his-name—Mr. Jones's—letter, and now I am ready to hear what you have to say."

But if he thought little of his visitor's appearance at first, he soon changed his sentiments toward him, for Tom had not spoken twenty words when Mr. Chillingsworth's whole aspect changed. He straightened himself up in his seat, laid aside his pipe, pushed away his glass of Madeira, and asked Tom to take a chair.

He listened without a word as Tom Chist told of the buried treasure, of how he had seen the black man murdered, and of how he and Parson Jones had recovered the chest again. Only once did Mr. Chillingsworth interrupt the narrative. "And to think," he cried, "that the villain this very day walks about New York town as though he were an honest man! But if we can only get hold of these log-books you speak of. Go on; tell me more of this."

When Tom Chist's narrative was ended, Mr. Chillingsworth's bearing was as different as daylight is from dark. He asked a thousand questions, all in the most polite and gracious tone imaginable, and not only urged a glass of his fine old Madeira upon Tom, but asked him to stay for supper. There was to be nobody there, he said, but his wife and daughter.

Tom, all in a panic at the very thought of the two ladies, sturdily refused to stay even for the cup of tea Mr. Chillingsworth offered him.

He did not know that he was destined to stay there as long as he lived.

"And now," said Mr. Chillingsworth, "tell me about yourself."

"I have nothing to tell, Your Honor," said Tom, "except that I was washed up out of the sea."

"Washed up out of the sea!" exclaimed Mr. Chillingsworth. "Why, how was that? Come, begin at the beginning, and tell me all."

Immediately Tom Chist did as he was asked, beginning at the very beginning, and telling everything just as Molly Abrahamson had often told it to him. As he continued, Mr. Chillingsworth's interest changed into an appearance of stronger and stronger excitement. Suddenly he jumped up out of his chair and began to walk up and down the room.

"Stop! Stop!" he cried out at last, in the midst of something Tom was saying. "Stop! Stop! Tell me; do you know the name of the vessel that was wrecked, and from which you were washed ashore?"

"I've heard it said," said Tom Chist, " 'twas the *Bristol Merchant*."

"I knew it! I knew it!" exclaimed the great man, in a loud voice, flinging his hands up into the air. "I felt it was so the moment you began the story. But tell me this, was there nothing found with you with a mark or a name upon it?"

"There was a kerchief," said Tom, "marked with a *T* and a *C*."

"Theodosia Chillingsworth!" cried out the merchant. "I knew it!

I knew it! Heavens! To think of anything so wonderful happening as this! Boy! Boy! Do you know who you are? You are my own brother's son. His name was Oliver Chillingsworth, and he was my partner in business, and you are his son." Then he ran out into the entryway, shouting and calling for his wife and daughter to come.

So Tom Chist—or Thomas Chillingsworth, as he was now to be called—did stay for supper, after all.

This is the story, and may it have pleased you. For Tom Chist became rich and great, as was to be supposed, and he married his pretty cousin Theodosia (who had been named for his own mother, drowned in the *Bristol Merchant*).

He did not forget his friends, but arranged that Parson Jones could come to New York to live.

As to Molly and Matt Abrahamson, they both enjoyed a pension of eighty pounds a year for as long as they lived; for now that all was well with him, Tom bore no grudge against the old fisherman for all the drubbings he had suffered.

The treasure-box was brought to New York, and if Tom Chist did not get all the money there was in it (as Parson Jones had thought he would), he got at least a good big lump of it.

And it is probable that those log-books did more to get Captain Kidd arrested in Boston town and hanged in London than anything else that was brought up against him.